BEST MICROFICTION

2025

Series Editors

Meg Pokrass, Gary Fincke

Guest Editor

Dawn Raffel

BEST MICROFICTION 2025
978-1-949790-98-6   Paperback
978-1-949790-99-3   Ebook

First Pelekinesis Printing 2025

For information:

Pelekinesis
112 Harvard Ave #65
Claremont, CA 91711 USA
ISSN 2641-9750

www.pelekinesis.com

*Best
Microfiction
2025*

BEST MICROFICTION ANTHOLOGY SERIES

Series Editors
Meg Pokrass, Gary Fincke

Guest Editor
Dawn Raffel

Copy Editor
Angeline Schellenberg

Interview Editor
Kathryn Kulpa

Production Editor
Cooper Renner

Layout and Design
Mark Givens

Cover illustration
Terry M. Givens

TABLE OF CONTENTS

ESSAYS & INSIGHTS

Introduction

DAWN RAFFEL, GUEST EDITOR

You hold in your hands a constellation of stories, each self-contained yet ineffably connected to its neighbors. Varying widely in style and expression, these 81 pieces share extreme compression, each one offering a shimmering glimpse of what it is to be alive in the world.

The paradox of microfiction is that rather than being confining, compression masterfully handled is abundantly spacious, inviting formal innovation and suggestion, precision and ambiguity. Every word matters, as does every word withheld, every space left trustingly open for the reader to imagine, to dream, to question, and to be moved in ways that defy explanation.

To all of the winners and finalists: Congratulations on packing so much life—and so much of the mystery of life–into so few words. And to everyone reading: I hope you find yourself as delighted, challenged, and inspired as I did.

BEST MICROFICTION

Communio Sanctorum

STEVE ALMOND

When the avalanche came, the fuselage filled with snow, like a throat. There were 24 people inside, survivors of a plane crash high in the Andes, boys mostly, rugby players buoyant with youth. They had shy girlfriends and old cars they shined by hand. They hung cigarettes from their lips and blew smoke at the sun. At night, their mothers stole into their rooms to watch them sleep. Some weeks ago, they had begun to eat the flesh of their dead comrades.

And now this: a wave of snow erasing them. For a few moments, there was absolute silence. A few began to moan. It was easier when they stopped struggling. One boy said later he could see a crown of light bending towards him. Another said he felt, at the moment of surrender, a tranquility so profound it would haunt him the rest of his life. A third— the one who came closest to dying—saw a hundred images from his childhood. He inspected them with great patience, like photographs, falling backward in time until he was just a baby on a white rug and his mother was walking towards him.

The boys were devout Catholics. They had been

raised to gaze upon their Redeemer as a man nailed to wood, His arms flung out for a bloody hug. Now they knew the truth. It was better than any vision. This is why, when they felt hands clutching at them, they fought to remain still. They were as spirits roused from the tomb of paradise. They smelled the stinking pleas of their bodies. Life hovered over them, a bully with the wild eyes of saints, pounding at their hearts, saving them.

Steve Almond is the author of twelve books of fiction and non-fiction, most recently *Truth Is the Arrow, Mercy Is the Bow*.

I Ask My Doctor Not to Pray for Me

Nin Andrews

My doctor worries when I tell him I am an atheist. He informs me that devout patients suffer less and have higher survival rates; I should learn to get down on my knees. On his wall is a picture of Jesus, his long strawberry blond locks falling forward, his blue eyes downcast, as if lost in thought or time or maybe a dialog with the bearded god in the clouds. His face is familiar, but I can't quite place him. Then I remember—he was in my high school class though he was held back a few years—a sixties flower child, Vietnam war protestor who smoked pot, played the guitar, and hung out with the fast crowd and never gave me a second glance. Years later I read that he was one of the boytoys for our parish priest, Father Thomas, who was known for offering spiritual direction to troubled youth. I want to ask if he's okay now, but he's wrapped in a sorrow so deep, no words rise from his throat.

Nin Andrews is the author of fifteen collections of poetry. Her poetry has been translated into Turkish, performed in Prague, and anthologized in England, Australia, and Mongolia. Her collection, *Son of a Bird*, a memoir in prose poems, will be published in 2025. For more information, visit her website: Ninandrews.com

Crossing Margo's Larder Off Your Bucket List

MIKKI ARONOFF

Margo's Larder is the most celebrated larder on the Trail of Crumbs and no wonder. Margo was born to flourishes, ejected with a crescendo the night the river flooded. And to fulsomeness, like her full-bosomed mother, a baker of madeleines and macaroons, whose lover, the butcher, kept his gluttonous thumbs on a scale sticky with sausage casings.

Margo's Larder is secret until you blow your bonus on a ticket. You can't stop grinning as guides usher you past cupboards that can't shut for jam jars and ant bait traps, past pantry shelves creaking and moaning with BOGO overflow. Her larder is Rubens and Rembrandt. A water-swoll camel. Scarlatti and Handel. A puffy pig. Your chef-y grail. Hold onto your stub, follow what sags to enter the sanctum. Behold, then, the chambers, the four-poster that sways with the spread of Margo in the flesh, dipping turkey quills in squid ink, scratching lengthy grocery lists onto vellum.

Margo will tire of the task. She will set her scrolls

aside, then give you a glance. This is only temporary, and you don't have much time. You stutter your devotion. She extends a limp hand and her remaindered book, which she will gladly sign. But first, you must hoick and hitch the billowing edges of her culinary promises. It is not unlike struggling with unruly sheets. But you've been practicing for weeks. She regards the width of your fingers. A simple dip of her chins signals success. Margo pats a corner of her bed for you to sit, lays out your portion of morning's sweet spoils. You can't believe you've made it this far. You tilt your toque, unpack your cutlery, tuck a napkin in your collar.

Mikki Aronoff writes tiny stories and advocates for animals. Her work has been long-listed for the *Wigleaf* Top 50 and nominated for Pushcart, Best of the Net, Best Small Fictions, Best American Short Stories, and Best Microfiction. Mikki has stories in *Best Microfiction 2024* and in *Best Small Fictions 2024*. She lives in New Mexico.

The Princess of Tides

AMY BARNES

Alice lives in the in-between spaces, a mouse of a mousy woman the size of a breath mint or a breath, hiding herself at the moment before dramatic music echoes a few notes on a *name that song* game show or when a car flirts with another one for an instant on the interstate or when two strangers see each other for the first time across a crowded room with obligatory smoke in their eyes. When she moves to the beach into a tiny rented house that is too trendy and expensive, but also as far as she can walk to the ocean, and she needs that - there's little left of her - a left brow and a left elbow stand out under blue dotted swiss and a slightly-dotty smile. Both of those features on the right side have evaporated because of the chemicals she is force fed three days a week with a side of Red Queen cards that Lewis ripple-shuffles because he used to be a Vegas croupier before they both jumped down the oncology rabbit hole of hard plastic chairs and hard plastic tubes. *The beach will be kind to us* Alice says to Lewis and the Thursday nurse who brings her warm honey buns and the *good* Jello, well-loved paperbacks and paper cups of tea with little notes on top that say *eat me* written in neat scrolling nurse script. Alice measures the days by the tide's arrival and departures, in and out, like the music of the machines that whir and surf and tide in the sterile blue room that smells like ocean because the Monday nurse sells essential oils and wax melts in *Ocean Breeze*. The Monday multiple level marketing would usually anger Alice, but she hides in the artificial waves that hide her waves of nausea. *Do you have that lovely smell in a candle too?* Alice asks Monday Nurse, the one who wears red scrubs and mahogany hair, and before she knows it, she's ordered a sample box of all things *Ocean Breeze.* Monday Nurse smiles and adds the form to her clipboard. When the box arrives a week later, Alice shrinks back into the space between the hotel ocean painting and Lewis' now-vacant chair, holding her candle tightly.

Amy Barnes has words at *Smokelong Quarterly*, *The Rumpus*, *X-R-A-Y Literary Magazine*, *-ette review*, and many other sites. Her writing was long-listed for the *Wigleaf* Top 50, 2021-2024, and included in *The Best Small Fictions 2022*. She's a *Fractured Lit* associate editor, *Gone Lawn* co-editor, *Ruby Lit* assistant editor, and *Narratively* chief submissions reader.

Moonlit Fields

ANDREW BERTAINA

And the train cutting through the fields, which were flooded with moonlight, and the dark shapes of the trees, making a small wind break beyond, and the way his mind swayed in quiet rhythm with the train and all of the things he was now forgetting about his mother who was gone, and just the train and the moonlit fields now, where once, he'd had a mother, who read to him at night, night after night, her voice curling around the words, so much like the quiet rhythm of the train, which carried him through the flooded fields and back into his childhood, which he missed so much, not the specific things anymore, but just the way his mother's voice carried him into sleep, and the way he used to stay awake at his window, and watch the white orb of the moon hung in the trees, and the sound of the grasshoppers in the wet grass, and nameless insects whirring in the trees and all that was passing now as the train rolled along, and he thought he could see, in the nameless fields, a glimpse of his childhood self, somewhere across the distant fields, in a window, illuminated, a square of light, and a child watching the night gather in the trees, and that nameless child thinking, as he thought, of how the darkness, if his mother was near, did not scare him, but made him feel that to be alone was safe, was good, was the shape of a life to come.

Andrew Bertaina is the author of the essay collection, *The Body Is A Temporary Gathering Place* (Autofocus 2024), and the short-story collection, *One Person Away From You* (Moon City Press Award Winner 2021). His work has appeared in *The Threepenny Review*, *New Letters*, *Prairie Schooner*, *Witness*, and elsewhere.

Rosetta Post-Its

GUY BIEDERMAN

Los Gatos Tienen Hambre, says the post-it on the fridge.

Since when did the cats learn Spanish, since when did they learn to write?

The same could be asked of you, says another post-it.

You tighten the belt on your bathrobe. You were House Samurai in a previous life, but the cats as writers, now roommates who borrow your stuff and leave snarky notes?

Stick to what you know, says a post-it: *thank you-notes, grocery lists, and poems that rhyme with dime. Leave speculative fiction to the pros.*

You take back your pen. The post-its you stole from work sit on the counter with notes in languages you don't even speak —

Anymore . . . says a post-it, claw and ink.

A black tail curls from under the curtain.

Two orange ears rise pyramid-like from behind the microwave.

You pull out organic turkey burgers and sprinkle

carefully clipped kitty grass onto bite-sized morsels placed on heirloom plates... and write your own post-it: *Satisfied*?!

You find your favorite mug and reach for Mr. Coffee.

Such a good boy, says a post-it on the sugar bowl in what must be cuneiform.

And how you know this, you dare not ask.

Btw, you're out of cream.

Guy Biederman is the author of *Translated From The Original: One-inch Punch Fiction* (Black Lawrence Press) and five other books of short work. He divides his time between a houseboat in Sausalito, an adobe in El Paso, an old cabin in Ruidoso New Mexico, and the roads in between.

Umami

Shlagha Borah

Silver, gleaming – the dead river fish in my father's hands. He holds it up like a trophy for the photograph. He adjusts its head on the bothi, gently scraping the scales off its back. Oil sizzles in the kitchen, mortar and pestle brimming with the paste of mustard seeds. I inherited the staleness of desire from him. In America, I cut open the pack of refrigerated tilapia, season it with ginger garlic paste. This is muscle memory – to touch what is raw and open. I marinate it in yogurt, sprinkle paprika all over its moist body. The wetness of fish alive in the tip of my fingers. The first time I picked out a fish bone, it pricked my forefinger. The blood mixed with the rice and my father joked how it enhanced the taste of the fish curry. We keep fish bones in a glass jar. My father's dying wish is to eat Sitol fish – a rare delicacy in our Rohu-Bhokua household. To separate the bones one by one, like strands of hair parted for a French braid. What doesn't have a name doesn't exist. My father slices its throat. The fish flaps its tail.

Shlagha Borah is from Assam, India. Her work appears in *The Cincinnati Review*, *The Florida Review*, and elsewhere. She's a 2024 Ruth Lilly and Dorothy Sargent Rosenberg Poetry Fellowship finalist and 2025 Miami Book Fair Poetry Emerging Writer Fellow. Her work has been supported by Brooklyn Poets, The Hambidge Center, Virginia Center for the Creative Arts, etc.

It Was a Year

KELLI SHORT BORGES

of Gloria Vanderbilts, a year of Farrah-feathered hair, a year of roller skates. A year of singing the Tab Cola theme song in bedrooms with pink canopy beds and clove cigarettes tucked deep inside ballerina music boxes. A year we still gripped our mothers' hands crossing streets while men smoking on corners watched, their eyes inhaling our mothers and exhaling us.

It was a year of lavender eyelids, of Love's Baby Soft, of training bras. A year of slumber parties and pillow fights, our cherry Lip-Smacker-ed lips puckered, suspended. A year of watching our mothers Jazzercise, their Jane-Fonda-starved bodies teaching us to watch our figures, teaching us our worth.

It was a year we giggled behind Trapper-Keepers while P.E. teachers taught us about periods and ovaries and menstrual pads and the pain that would make us women. A year we wondered, when that pain stole our breath, why our mothers had never warned us.

It was a year of Orange Crush and crushes and being crushed on by boys named Rob and Dan and John, the words "sperm" and "sex" and "hard-on" foreign fruit on our tongues. A year of spin-the-bottle, of wanting, searching, fumbling. A year of losing ourselves in darkened corners of darkened basements with our mothers still in the dark.

It would be years before learning we belonged to the world, to men on corners inhaling us, exhaling our mothers. Years before we would call to the ghosts of the girls we were, *come back, come back, come back.*

Kelli Short Borges writes from her home in Phoenix, Arizona. Her stories appear in *Lost Balloon*, *Sky Island Journal*, *Ghost Parachute*, *Peatsmoke*, and *Fictive Dream*, among other journals. Recently, her work was chosen for the *Wigleaf* Top 50 longlist and *Best Microfiction 2024*. She is currently working on her first novel.

Bug Facts

TIMOTHY BOUDREAU

Tomorrow you'll look up how caterpillars pee and what kind of spiders are big enough to eat birds and why a dragonfly would want to fly backward.

It's sleepover weekend. The five-year-old can't know how much pain you or your wife are in, the thick ribbon of scar under the partially peeled layer of your surgical glue, the hip your wife tweaked, or is it arthritis, the doctors can't decide.

When you go upstairs you'll be sleeping alone, but it's fine, it's just the arrangement. She sets up the spare bedroom, joins your grandson there; she likes it better, it gives you some space, at least one of you may get a decent night's sleep.

She'll sleep with her body curled toward her grandson, the ceiling fan blowing the silver-blond of her bangs. She won't sleep until he does, which won't happen till he talks himself out, tall tales and sleepy ones, tales from the big book on the shelf beside the bed, the spiders, honeybees and dragonflies filling his head as he lies back, facing the ceiling, eyelids fluttering shut.

Upstairs you'll sleep the untroubled sleep of the sufficiently drugged. You'll be first up in the morning, and after you make breakfast and cuddle your grandson on the couch, you'll Google his insect questions from the night before. When your wife rouses herself from the spare bedroom, your grandson will run bright-eyed to her with his newest bug facts.

You and the five-year-old will carry the conversation. Your wife will sip her coffee and watch the boy, beam at him, in fact. She will not make eye contact with you.

Caterpillars don't pee but they poop all the time, black blotches on perfectly green leaves. A giant South American spider eats hummingbirds, lizards, and rodents, injects them with poison before drinking their insides, leaves the husks of the corpses behind. Some dragonflies prefer to fly backwards to visit the places they've already been, maybe they think there are happier times back then, something magical before everything started to go wrong.

Timothy Boudreau lives in northern New Hampshire. His novel *All We Knew Were Our Hearts* is due from ELJ Editions in 2026. He is an editor at *The Loveliest Review*. Find him on BlueSky at @tcboudreau or at timothyboudreau.com

Shape-shifting for beginners

ANGELITA LAPUZ BRADNEY

My daughter tells me she's a cat. I am not her mother anymore, she says, because I'm human and she is not. She wears ears and a tail, insists others don't understand. Others including me. She doesn't know how I fought like a tiger when she was bullied in the playground for the colour of her skin. She doesn't remember how, to get her to sleep, I carried her in a kangaroo pouch and walked the night streets for hours while the moon glowed cold and the lights shone orange on the wet pavements. She doesn't recall the times I held her slippery, wriggling fish body in the bath, bubbles drifting around us. The evenings I crouched beside her, parting her hair with my fingers and combing out every louse with the dexterity of a chimpanzee. How in summer we pulled ripe cherries from the tree, popping them into our mouths with the greed of parakeets. How in winter we snuggled together like dormice in a den. How I fed her milk from my body. How I shielded her from the hyenas. How I taught her to use her voice, insistent as the call of an elephant, or a wolf, or a lion. And yes, to be as independent as a cat, so that nobody would ignore her wishes.

Angelita Lapuz Bradney's short fiction has won prizes and is published in journals such as *Litro*, *Fictive Dream*, and *Shooter Literary Magazine*. She is working on a novel based on British and Filipino folklore, which was shortlisted for the SI Leeds Literary Prize in 2024. www.angelitabradney.com

When the Dog Died

LEONE BRANDER

When the dog died we didn't know what to do. We had nowhere to put him and the ground was too frozen to dig a hole. Cremation was $700, which was more than we had. We worried terribly about it. Could we thaw the earth somehow? Could we take him to a farm? Was there enough wood for a tiny coffin? The first time someone suggested the garbage bin out back we all shuddered. There was no dignity in that. The dog deserved more, surely. We loved him, you see. We loved him like one of us. But our choices evaporated as fast as a drop of water on hot cast iron. There wasn't enough money, or wood, or dirt. Then someone pointed out how much the dog had always loved garbage, how he was always sneaking fish bones or watermelon rinds or dirty paper towels when we weren't watching. Once we'd forgotten to tie the full bag tight enough, and returned home in the evening to find black plastic shreds strewn across the lawn and the dog on his back squirming through old coffee grounds and kitchen scraps. We could only laugh. Look how alive and happy our dog is, we'd said. Wouldn't life be better if we could roll through the garbage so freely? So that decided it. We wrapped him in old towels and kissed his soft head and placed him in the garbage bin outside. We recited a hymn. All week we walked past him and left gifts. Here is an apple core. Here is a tinfoil ball full of bacon grease. Finally, on Monday, one of us wheeled him to the curb. No one was home when the garbage truck came, so when we returned in the evening the bin was empty and we couldn't bear it. We filled it with things we never planned on throwing away, things we realized we didn't need. An umbrella. Old issues of National Geographic. A set of hair rollers. Someone even tossed in their new collared shirt. We were like children, throwing toys in a toybox. And from then on, every piece of trash felt like a prayer. Turkey neck. Old shoe. Napkin.

Leone Brander (she/her) is a writer and artist from the Canadian prairies. She holds an MFA from Boston University. Her work has appeared in *Grain*, *the Texas Review*, *THIS*, and elsewhere. @leonebrander on all platforms.

Dangling over the Sea

NICOLE BROGDON

Lucky me, my first whiff of death came late, at twenty-five, me leading lipsticked Grandma Lorena by the elbow on west Galveston Island, guiding her through the crowd toward the outdoor musical seats— "South Pacific"— while she clutched my upper arm with one hand, balancing her strawberry red wig on her head with another, her body smelling of leaked urine, *Coty* face powder, and *Jungle Gardenia*, our bellies full of Landry's fried fish and whiskey old fashioneds with maraschino cherries, followed by key lime pie, our clothes sparkly, moods high, since we knew all the flirty lyrics and we hummed our way through the acts standing clapping then finally shuffling toward the car, her death-gripping my arm because her mother-in-law Betty fell years ago and, "Well, that was the end of Betty," me driving us—my upper arm, sore—home along the Seawall beneath a giant crescent moon, yellow tip pointed like a fishhook that could pierce our mouths, catch us, dangle us, and drop us, *splash*, over the Gulf while Grandma, the old bargirl once famous for men's hats and bare legs, riding shotgun and looking tiny, rotting fruit from body cavities flavoring the air, her voice gravelly from chain smoking, her face turned toward the waves, told me again, how she used to work at *The Chinese Duck* during Prohibition, "Right at the end of that pier, was a long building with a hinged floor at the back, so when a cop came in, we could spread the news mouth to mouth all the way back, to lift the floor and hide the booze," and she asked me again, "Did you ever make love in the ocean, Honey?" and I didn't answer, then she said, softer, "I want you to know, I don't recall a finer evening in my entire life," and me feeling sad sadness like humidity, driving my rusty Toyota through the moonlit night with my cargo, the wild sea sloshing nearby, for the very last time.

Nicole Brogdon is an Austin TX trauma therapist interested in strugglers and stories, with fiction in *Vestal Review*, *Cleaver*, *Flash Frontier*, *Bending Genres*, *Bright Flash*, *South Florida Poetry Journal*, *Cafe Irreal*, *101Words*, *Centifictionist*, and *Best Microfiction 2024*. Twitter @NBrogdonWrites! & nbrogdonwrites.bsky.social

The Devil You Don't Know

MELISSA LLANES BROWNLEE

The devil will enter your body if you sleep with your feet to the door. He likes to hop in bodies. He knows how easy it is, especially with girls like you, my mother warns as she pulls my ponytail tight, brush bristles scraping my scalp, revenge for all of the ukus she had to comb out and wash too many times with the uku shampoo.

The devil enters bodies. He likes children who don't listen. Children who don't cook the rice when they get home. Children who watch TV and don't clean the bathroom or wash their laundry before their mothers get home, she yells, clutching the wooden spoon in her hand.

The devil likes bodies, especially bodies like yours that should be hidden, covered.

The devil wants to enter your body, she whispers as she moves your bed so your feet face the door, *because he knows what kind of girl you are.* You can't move. She's strapped you in tight, so the bed bugs don't bite, the edges of the sheet holding you down.

The devil enters your body as she watches, the

triumph ablaze in her eyes. He enters through your toes. You can feel a warmth spread upwards, a fiery hug of nerve endings and muscle fibers. He moves slow, in time to your heart, slowing your breath, calming you. You watch her triumph die as the devil smiles with your lips and you join him with your eyes.

Melissa Llanes Brownlee (she/her), a native Hawaiian writer living in Japan, has work in *Wigleaf* and *Cutleaf*. Read *Hard Skin* (2022) and *Kahi and Lua* (2022) and look out for *Bitter over Sweet* (November 2025) from Santa Fe Writers Project. She tweets @lumchanmfa and talks story at melissallanesbrownlee.com

Afterlife for Rent

KATI BUMBERA

Sometimes, in stiff-necked, midweek snooze-button dreams, it turns out that Dad is still alive. I find him towering in the kitchen, wearing that green cardigan, waiting to catch me out just like when I was young, when I'd come home from school and I'd be forced to walk past him, risking his glare, if I wanted anything, like a snack from the fridge, a Nirvana t-shirt, or a boyfriend, or a lift to the train station where I eventually left him. He waved me off in that same cardigan, the scratchy strands of childhood already fraying in a new light.

And now he's here. But this time round, almost as old as Dad was on that platform, I am the one who looks askance at promises and late arrivals. His cardigan snags on rusty memories of hospitals and graveyards, threatening to unravel the fragile dream. I don't believe in robins on windowsills. I know he isn't bringing wisdom, I know he hasn't come to seek forgiveness.

And then I think, maybe he's not here for me at all. I can just leave him, one more time, to have his kitchen to himself and be a little bit alive. Sit by a window, listen to dust carts empty the bins. There's beer in the fridge, Dad, I say to him, then turn around and tiptoe back into the light.

Kati Bumbera is a short fiction writer with work published in *Apex Magazine, DarkWinter Literary Magazine, Best Microfiction 2024,* and various online journals. She lives in France, where she works as a video games writer and tinkers endlessly with the first chapter of her debut novel.

Clara Schumann Washing Dishes

LATON CARTER

Sometimes I think of all the people I'll never know. Even now someone is kneeling. Not worship, but praying for a line to follow. My life is full. Seven children, and I look at my hands—proud and large. But Johannes, when something is insistently absent— the tongue travels to the missing tooth. We try to heal ourselves, conjure distractions. In the meantime, I remember everything. February, sleet, inside a mind devouring itself, our Robert on the bridge—it made sense to him. *Not* dying didn't make sense. And the fisherman who pulled him out, still alive—picture the dinner table stories. A half-frozen man in robe and slippers, boxing his own ears and spitting letters. Now I perform his music in place of my own. I oblige my travel and mentor duties.

In St. Petersburg I rode to the palace in a sled. The samovar held tea to warm my hands. Back home, you were doing something—holding your fists behind your back, waiting for the continent to move. A life heavy with patience is still a life. There's no distance when my eyes close and yours emerge. We both know how to suffer. Some days I lose all ability with meaning, every phrase a clot. Nothing adds up. I know men are different animals. It scares me to think of all the diversions. The brain must be a monstrous thing— too powerful for the pliant ways of the body. Still, think of me. Ice does not last forever.

Laton Carter's short fiction has appeared in *The Boiler*, *Indiana Review*, *Necessary Fiction*, *New Flash Fiction Review*, and other journals. Carter works in a middle school in Western Oregon.

Mary

CHRISTINE H. CHEN

When we moved in, Ah Ma told Ba to remove the shrine outside. It was a statuette of the Virgin Mary inside a dome, pink-cheeked, clad in azure blue, arms outstretched, gazing down to wilted roses in tiny white vases. Ah Ba pulled, dragged, pushed. The base wouldn't budge. Ah Ma came out with hammers, but we children stood in front of the helpless Mary. *Sacrilege*, my older brother said. *You and your gwei-lo education!* Ah Ma wagged her hammers at us, *this is nonsense, you hear me?* Ah Ba went to Home Depot, came back with rhododendron bushes he planted around Mary. Inside, we laid steamy sweet buns and roasted pork in our ancestral altar, we held burning incense and bowed to sculpted names of our ancestors. Ah Ma and Ba poured rice wine on the floor. Ah Ma prayed for protection for our first home, for us the family here, and for the one left behind in China. Ma planted tomatoes, squashes, and green beans in the yard, away from the blooming rhododendrons where Mary stayed hidden, stoic under rain, in scorching heat, or wrapped in snow as time wore on. Ma grew old and arthritic, the vegetable gardens yellowed and drooped to the ground. The year Ah Ba died, a snowstorm blew a broken tree into our yard, missed my older brother's head by a few feet as he was rushing to the garage. Mary deflected the blow. She lay on the snow, feet broken off from the cement base, her dome shattered in two pieces. Ah Ma picked her up, carried her to the kitchen sink, let warm water shower the snow away. She swept a soap-sudded sponge over Mary's face over and over.

Where is Home?

CHRISTINE H. CHEN

Is it the smell of fried fish balls, of soft tofu
simmered with scallions in bone broth, the hubbub
of the midnight merchants shouting their offerings
to the wind while you stare at the scintillating lights
on the streets down below from a Hong Kong high-
rise window, wishing you were old enough to stay
up late like the Ma-Jong players, or the African
sun on your face, your steps on the sand the color
of rust you tread carefully to avoid the mound the
pyramid ants built, the puff of dust you kick to
scatter chickens and crows swirling above a holed
up carcass, the shadow of a baobab tree, a sudden
drop of rain on your nose, your Ma's shouting, *get
back right now*, then you remember the drying bed
sheets and clothes in the backyard, and rush to help
your Ba unpin and grab them instead, or the blanket
of fog swaddling the Golden Gate bridge on your
morning Sunday runs from the university campus,
the steam rising from onions and hot pots drifting
from Chinatown you return to over and over again,
letting yourself submerge in nostalgic scents, biting
on tapioca pearls swimming in milk, or the maple

tree turning blood red in your garden behind your New England cottage when the crisp Autumn air hit, the crinkling of a rug of oak leaves under your boots when you fail to catch the sight of a cardinal standing still for a breath as elusive as home?

Born in Hong Kong and raised in Madagascar before settling in Boston where she worked as a chemist, **Christine H. Chen** has fiction in *SmokeLong Quarterly*, *Time & Space Magazine*, *Fractured Lit*, and other journals and anthologies. She is a recipient of the 2022 Mass Cultural Council Artist Fellowship. www.christinehchen.com

Breaking Bread

Kim Chinquee

My dad sits in a greenhouse, glowing in the dark. He says, Pass the peas.

I see his brain light up like crosswalks I hardly saw in childhood, having grown up on a farm, though I imagine the crosswalks of his brain, all the different voices, and I wonder, if his voices have a color, would they be bright and neon? Or like death, the fall? Pastel, maybe gentle? Do the voices shout or whisper? Do they laugh like he sometimes did out of the blue, as if he had a secret? Or do they yell the way he yelled at me when I was just a girl and cried because I had a headache or a cough or was scared and felt I had to vomit? Do his voices make him scared? After he died, when I went to clean out his apartment, a medical card was in his wallet saying he was paranoid. A schizophrenic.

I knew something was wrong, but I never knew his diagnosis. My mom left him when I was young, and after that my dad's parents said I was a sinner. They put me on a ride and left me spindling. They said to be ashamed. They said they had no doubt. Later, as I grew into an adult, I tried to reach my dad. My grandparents wouldn't let me, and then they died, leaving me with nothing.

My dad couldn't hold a conversation. He was at a halfway house and when I tried to visit, sometimes he shut the door, sometimes he stood there, staring at me, crying. His eyes looked absent, sometimes mad. Sometimes I feared that he would break me.

Now he wears sweatpants in the color of his farm clothes. Gray and forest green. A shade between the two, and he wears a pearl necklace, an heirloom I have in my jewelry box that was gifted to me when my aunt died. There's a tattoo of an ax on his forehead. He spins his chair, leaning himself backwards. He says, The loquats here are square and dull. He says, Up here, the snow shines and it makes the sky melt.

He burps. He farts. He laughs and hands me a bread loaf and says, Say hi to god. He says, I dare you to break it. I dare you to eat it. I dare you to feel.

Kim Chinquee's eighth book is *Pipette*, a novel. Her collections *Contact With the Wild* and *Octopus Arms* (MadHat Press) and novella *I Thought of England* (Baobab Press) are forthcoming. She's a three-time Pushcart Prize recipient. She edits for *New World Writing Quarterly*, *Elm Leaves Journal*, and *Midwest Review*, and lives in Buffalo, NY

Somewhere, Deep inside her Lacrimals, Something is Blocking Cora's Tears.

Hayli May Cox

Cremated fingernails or white lily pollen or the dust of tissues at a hundred funerals—though nobody she's loved has ever died. The mites around her eyes are not doing their job, and she pictures them sleeping at the tips of her lashes rather than dead or gone because she doesn't understand loss enough to imagine it. Cora's eyes remain dry, lids sticking audibly, until she tips her chin up to the florescent lights of her apartment bathroom and lets Visine drip in twos and threes. When she is anxious, she picks at the inside corners of her eyes until they bleed—something wet to wash away the dust.

Cora hasn't cried for nearly two decades. Not since before she could read, and not after the first laws mandating funerals for aborted and miscarried fetuses. It had seemed like everyone was grieving something back then. Her uncle was a funeral director and her father a self-proclaimed entrepreneur, so to make extra money they listed Cora's services at funerals—some smaller echo of professional mourners from cultures older than their own. Cora became a checkbox on a

41

form for additional options, right below "electronic memory board". For two years she floated fairy-like about those heavy rooms as great aunts crooned their necks and grieving mothers lifted her into their laps, drying wet cheeks with her toddler curls.

Now, Cora eats hot peppers, cuts boiler onions dangerously close to her face. She watches *Bridge to Terabithia* and *Marley & Me*, but she's never had a sister or a dog so these do nothing for her. She takes a bath with the lights off until her palms wrinkle. She lets the water drain around her as she feels the weight of herself slowly return. She thinks of the saddest moments of her life. When her apartment manager discovered her cat and forced her to return him to the shelter after she'd raised him from a kitten. Her father's face when she dropped out of grad school. Yesterday, when her girlfriend packed up to move to Colorado and told Cora she was nothing but hollow inside. Cora lies at the bottom of the tub, and even with her hair spidered around her shoulders and water pooled in her bellybutton, she feels wrung dry. She picks the scabs around her eyes, lubricating.

Hayli May Cox holds a PhD from The University of Missouri and is Assistant Professor of Creative Writing at Waldorf University. A Michigander by birth, in her free time Hayli paints, builds LEGO worlds, critter watches, and hikes around with her little, leggy dog.

Pet Shop Boys

TIM CRAIG

Dayne's on-off-off-on stepdad, Kel, says stay away from that new pet shop.

He says, what's a Pakistani want with opening a pet shop in this town anyway? There's something not right about that, I'm telling you.

He's not Pakistani, we say; he's Afghan.

What's that got to do with the price of custard creams? Kel says, pulling the ring on another Stella.

But you might as well tell a nail to stay away from a magnet as tell the three of us to stay away from a pet shop, especially when the only other places still open on the high street are two hairdressers, the Sue Ryder and a vape shop, and we're banned from all of them.

So we go into the pet shop after school every day and we try to teach the African Grey parrot to say fuck off and we tap on the glass of the snake's tank, the one with the sign that says Do Not Tap on Glass.

And we learn that he is called Shahmeer — the owner not the snake — and he tells us that in his language this means 'very handsome', and he laughs when he says it and we see his black tooth, which is minging.

And sometimes he lets us hold the hamsters and the gerbils if we're careful, and other times he brings out this little tray of sweet, colored cakes and we stuff our face with them, just like the hamsters, and they're the best thing ever but we say, no wonder your teeth are fucking black Shahmeer, and we ask if we can give a bit of cake to the big black rabbit but he says no, so we do it anyway.

And one day after school we head down the High Street as usual and we see the big front window of the shop is boarded up and there's broken glass inside and someone has sprayed the word PAEDO on the door in red and we stand there in the drizzle and share a damp ciggie and say, yeah – what did he want with opening a pet shop in this town anyway?

Originally from Manchester, **Tim Craig** lives in London. His micro stories have appeared several times previously in *Best Micro-fiction* and his debut collection *Now You See Him* is available from Ad Hoc Fiction.

Stuck

KAREN CRAWFORD

Our legs stick to the plastic-covered sofa. Shorts stick to our skin, heat sticks to our bangs, blinds stick to the windows to keep out the bugs, the soot, the air.

Granny calls our fingers sticky. Don't touch the yellowing photographs. Don't touch the candy-colored almonds. Don't touch the lace doilies or the porcelain figurines. Hands off the TV. Hands off each other. We stick together until my sister unglues. Peels away with a whimper, then whines.

We had a dog once. A dog that stuck by our side. A dog that bared its teeth at Mama's boyfriend. A dog that burrowed its nose in my hands. I bury my hands in my pockets. My sister pockets a dog figurine.

Granny smacks her dentures. Mama's boyfriend was a smacker. He talked smack, lip smacked, used smack. My sister smacks her gum. She's clutching the figurine. It slips from her hand smacking the floor.

Granny hunches over. She drags my sister into the bathroom and locks her inside. A growl is stuck in my throat. My legs unstick from the sofa, the heat still sticks to my bangs. My sister is pleading, my hands are sweating, I stick them against the shivering door.

Karen Crawford lives and writes in the City of Angels. Her work has been included in *National Flash Fiction Day Anthology 2024*, *Flash Boulevard*, *Okay Donkey*, *100 Words*, *Bending Genres*, and elsewhere. She is a multi-Pushcart, Best Microfiction and Best of the Net nominee.

Questions The Caseworker Should Have Asked After My Ex Accused Me of Neglect

BARBARA DIGGS

What's your child's name? What grade is she in? What's her daily routine? Does she brush her teeth every morning? Does she cry every night? What school does she go to? How are her grades? Have you observed behavioral changes? Does she startle at small noises? Flinch when classmates raise hands? Drop her books at the bell? What activities is she interested in? What are her favorite games? Is she good at hide and seek? Where does she hide when your ex hammers on the front door? Screams *I'ma fucking kill you* from the sidewalk? Does she prefer her bedroom closet or under the kitchen sink? How small can she shrink herself? Does she know how to fade into a sofa cushion? Become a fixture on a wall? Does she like to play tag? How fast can she run for help? What kind of chores does she do? Does she wash dishes? Mop your blood off the floor? Sweep broken plates, lamps, or teeth? How does she sleep at night? Does she wake up whimpering? Or does she cry soundlessly? How well did you explain the restraining order? Did she believe it when you swore it'd protect you? Did her eyes look so old that you felt like the child? How hard did you fight for sole custody? For supervised visitation? How shocked were you to learn she cuts herself before each visit? Makes Xs like tiny stars in the most tender part of her arm? What did she say when you swore he would never touch her? Did she tell you it's not your ex's hands she fears most? But that she might melt before his tear-stained apologies? Fall prey to his killer smile? The way you always did?

Barbara Diggs is a Washington, D.C., native and long-time resident of Paris, France. Her fiction has appeared in or is forthcoming in *Wigleaf*, *SmokeLong*, *Fractured Lit*, and *Your Impossible Voice*, and has won Highly Commended awards with The Bridport Prize and Bath Flash Fiction. Find her at bdiggswrites.bsky.social

The Tired Daughter

DARA YEN ELERATH

The tired daughter finds threads of insomnia in her soup, twisted among the bits of gristle and chicken. *What is this?* she asks the anxious mother. *It's nothing*, the mother replies, *eat your soup*, so the tired daughter sips the salty liquid. At night she cannot sleep. *Anxious mother*, she says, *what's wrong with me? When I close my eyes I feel I'm dying.* The anxious mother tries to calm her, *you'll fall asleep*, she says, *don't worry*, but the tired daughter watches the ceiling. She weeps.

She does not know her mother weaves sleeplessness into her water, into the sandwiches and nectarines she eats for lunch. She does not know her mother longs to loosen her skull like the lid of a jar and store her own anxieties inside: her fear of spiders and cars, her fear of cavities and cancer, her fear of old age and dying alone. *I have no other place to keep my worries*, the anxious mother moans. She goes to bed dreaming of how, instead of her, the tired daughter will carry the letters and postcards of anxiety, the ampoules and vials of doubt, the books and ency-clopediae of nervousness.

The tired daughter feels these things rattling inside her and can never fall asleep. Weeks of insomnia pass and the daughter longs for her mother to hold her. In her longing she grows roots and leaves. In her longing she becomes an apple tree. She spreads her arms into thick, gnarled branches, and the anxious mother plucks the fruit that dangles down. *These are sweet*, she says, forgetting her cares; *I like you this way*, she croons, watering her daughter daily.

In time, the daughter's apples will brown and rot. In time, worms will weave around the apple pips and stems, yet neither mother nor daughter guesses this now. They've found a way to live together peacefully. The daughter sprouts apples of forgetfulness and the mother eats them; as she eats she sings a lullaby. The daughter, heavy beneath her blanket of apples and song, grows tired; she ceases to speak. She slips into a deep, unknowing, apple-scented sleep.

Dara Yen Elerath's debut collection, *Dark Braid* (2020, BkMk Press), won the John Ciardi Prize for Poetry. Her work has appeared in journals such as *The Atlantic*, *The American Poetry Review*, *Poetry*, *High Country News*, *AGNI*, *New Flash Fiction Review*, *Wigleaf*, and elsewhere. She lives in Albuquerque, New Mexico.

Lookback Window
New York

PATRICIA ENGEL

after untitled drawing from *Studies* series
by Laylah Ali (U.S.A.) 2010-13

She tells me I am beautiful the same day he says
my face disgusts him. She tells me I am brilliant the
same day he tells me I am not as smart as I think I
am. She tells me I am a loving human being the same
day he tells me I am selfish and spiteful. She tells me
I am brave the same day he tells me I'm a coward.
She tells me I am a survivor, a hero, the same day he
tells me I am a viper, damaged, dead. Long ago he
made me think possession was union and union is
ownership and ownership requires loyalty and loyalty
is compliance; that a woman can be claimed like
land, a stake driven through her body's soil. Long
ago I learned silence is shelter and poison. I spoke in
broken sentences to sisters who heard the missing words
because they speak the same hushed dialect. There is
no endurance without the swell of time, the pressure
on the torso, the legs; grief's inertia. They are two
people: the he of then, the he of now. But they are the
same, demanding submission. Lookback window says

the Act, the pursuit of civil relief, a chance to review what memory made unspeakable; symbolic justice is no justice but light burns clear fire when pushed through glass. He stole my face. My original smile. I search for it in old clothing, photos, in portraits that were not hijacked, tainted, sabotaged. She tells me it's because he hates me that he treats me this way the same day he tells me it's because he loves me that he treats me this way. She tells me I can remember if I try hard and I can forget if I try harder. The lawyer wants dates, proof of conversations, those I briefed after the fact. But I told no one, not knowing there is a statute for sorrow, not knowing there is limitation to how long one may legally grieve their own passing. There is no secret diary, no hidden calendar. Court does not mean crime does not mean prison does not mean truth. The lawyer says you cannot attribute memories without witness, conversations without corroboration, you cannot remember certain things and forget others. You cannot summon a ghost to trial. You don't understand, I say. The ghost is me.

Patricia Engel is the author of five bestselling and award-winning works of fiction including, most recently, *Infinite Country* and *The Faraway World*. She is a professor of creative writing at the University of Miami.

Self-Portrait in the Time of Disaster

FEDERICO ESCOBAR

By noon I am done. I take the picture to her, up the stairs, past the living room, through the sleeping alligators, and she shakes her head again. "Not yet," she says, "not quite."

Undone, I come back to the studio, to the dark womb it is. I smash the palette against the wall, dim the lights. I fetch new oil paints, eat most of the green until I realize it's not red, and squeeze the paints onto a bone palette until the metal tubes slice my fingers.

I paint.

I paint.

I paint over the piece of canvas that was, for a few minutes, exactly what I wanted. I coat over it, with thick brushstrokes that add half an inch of oblivion. I close my eyes as the camel-hair brush swirls, and dances, sliding forward and back and back.

When the sun is done with people, I stare at the canvas and say, *Yes, this is her, this is finally her.* Most of the paint has dried tight between my fingers, wrinkled as if ages had passed.

By evening I am done. I take the picture to her, up the stairs, the living room draped in darkness, the snapping mouths of alligators imposing on my thoughts. She looks at a mirror, scans the painting, shakes her head. "Not quite," she says. "Still not me."

Federico Escobar is from Cali, Colombia. He has lived in New Orleans, Jerusalem, Oxford, and Puerto Rico, experiencing a hurricane, a couple of earthquakes, and plenty of rain along the way. He has been writing for a few decades and now works in education.

Cruel Choices

ALEXIS RHONE FANCHER

When my husband's two grown daughters are in
town, the three of them go to the movies, or play
pool. Share dinner every night. Stay out late. I haven't
seen my stepdaughters since my son's funeral in 2007.
When people ask, I say nice things about the girls, as
if we had a relationship. When people ask if *I* have
children I change the subject. Or I lie, and say no. Or
sometimes I put them on the spot and tell them yes,
but he died. They look aghast and want to know what
happened. Then I have to tell them about the cancer.
Sometimes, when the older daughter, his favorite, is
in town, and she and my husband are out together
night after night, I wonder what it would be like if
that was me, and my boy, if life was fair, and, rather
than my husband having two children and I, none,
we each had one living child. His choice which one
to keep. Lately when people ask, I want to lie and
say yes, my son is a basketball coach; he married a
beautiful Iranian model with kind eyes, and they
live in London with their twin girls who visit every
summer; the same twins his girlfriend aborted with
my blessing when my son was eighteen, deemed too

young for fatherhood, and everyone said there would be all the time in the world.

Alexis Rhone Fancher has authored ten books of poetry, most recently *Brazen* (NYQ), and *Triggered* (MacQ Press). She's published in *Best American Poetry, Rattle, Verse Daily, The American Journal of Poetry, Plume, Diode, Flock,* and elsewhere. She's a multiple Best of the Net and Pushcart Prize nominee. www.alexisrhonefancher.com

Plotting

GRANT FAULKNER

A wise writer once said that "the king died, and then the queen died," is a story, but that "the king died, and then the queen died of grief," now that was a plot, except the king died of a heart attack while in amorous congress with the queen's handmaiden, and the queen didn't know what was going on because she was doddling the exchequer, the exchequer who sired the handmaiden (but had nothing to do with the handmaiden's mother after the siring), but it was all alright because the king ruled by divine right, so neither he nor the queen really cared about plots too much, not when pleasures were at hand, and the queen was quite happy to rule over everybody with the power of God's blessings after her poor sick king's untimely death, that is until the exchequer poisoned her and told everyone how she'd been so terribly stricken with grief that she died of it, leaving the exchequer and the handmaiden free to abscond with a bag full of royal jewels and sail to France to live the louche life of happy libertines, proving that a libidinous nature and criminal proclivities can actually pay (although no one could explain why the exchequer disappeared without a trace soon afterward, or why the handmaiden said that her father had taught her everything she knew).

Grant Faulkner is the co-founder of *100 Word Story*, the co-host the *Write-minded* podcast, and an executive producer on *America's Next Great Author*. He has published several books, including *The Art of Brevity: Crafting the Very Short Story* and *Fissures*, a collection of 100-word stories, and his flash fiction has been widely anthologized.

I'm in Love with the Cave Man

Epiphany Ferrell

I've given my heart to the cave man. He walked into the Circle-K at the end of my shift. He bought a bundle of firewood and a gallon jug of tea. "I like your blue hair," he said to me. My hair is light brown. "I see potential," he said. "It's like seeing the future, but not a pristine view."

The cave man drives an old motorcycle. I ride in the sidecar. It's the only thing he got from his father — that and a tendency toward tendonitis and a whole lot of regret.

It's a nice cave. People have lived here before, a thousand years ago. I lie beside him on the furs that are his bed, and I look at the stars through the perfect circle on the roof of the cave, a hole that lets out the smoke and sometimes, if he forgets to cover it, lets in the rain. It's his modern addition, he says. We drink mushroom tea and listen to the frogs and the owls and the coyotes, and when I worry they are too close, he tells me to listen, that listening is medicine.

I walk the trail to his cave, picking flowers along

the way to give the cave a ladylike touch, to remind him I am his. When I arrive, I see that his furs are gone, his plank table is dismantled, his clay dishes shattered. There is a note, written on good paper with a fountain pen, not with charcoal, not in the dirt. There is no point even in reading it: I know I won't see him again.

Epiphany Ferrell's stories appear in more than 100 journals and anthologies, including *Best Microfiction*, *Best Small Fictions*, *Wigleaf*, *Ghost Parachute*, *Bending Genres*, and the anthology *Shakespeare Unleashed*. She lives near the Shawnee National Forest in Southern Illinois.

Sea Watchers

SARAH FRELIGH

after Edward Hopper

And still they come here every summer, same motel, same room. Each time, they unpack, backs to each other, change into bathing suits and walk to the beach. He sits like a lifeguard, alert to any movement. She closes her eyes and remembers the man who begged her to leave her marriage, the man who'd seen the shadow around her, nothing good in her future. And nothing was, nothing was ever good again, and so they come back here each summer to wait for what will never wash up. Think of bones bleached by salt water, the insistence of a small child to *look at me daddy, mommy, watch me.*

Sarah Freligh is the author of seven books, including *Sad Math*, winner of the 2014 Moon City Press Poetry Prize, and *Hereafter*, winner of the 2024 Bath Novella-in-Flash contest. Among her awards are poetry fellowships from the National Endowment for the Arts and the Saltonstall Foundation.

Sleepwalking

JEFF FRIEDMAN

My lover sleepwalks after midnight, leaving a trail of open doors behind her. If I clasp her arm to bring her back, she stops momentarily to lift my hand off and continues on as if I had never touched her. She has yet to fall down steps or stumble on the sidewalk. She parts the night as if wading through shallow water. When a car comes, she waits on the corner. Sometimes I walk beside her to see the brightness of her face as if the moon is lighting it. "Where are we going," I ask. "I'll know when we get there," she answers, but she's not awake. And sometimes I follow her to see if she will wait for me, but she just keeps going, no matter how far I fall behind. At such times, I hurry to catch up, fearing that a tree might reach for her with its long limbs or a dark bird might snatch her with its beak or the chunks of a dying star might crash down on her, but nothing like that happens. Instead, she stops and gathers the wind in her mouth, blowing into the darkness until it is even darker. Then she follows the shadows through the open doors, and I close them behind her.

Jeff Friedman has published eleven collections of poetry and prose, including his most recent, *Broken Signals* (Bamboo Dart Press). His work has appeared in *Best Microfiction*, *The New Republic*, *Flash Fiction Funny*, *Poetry*, and *American Poetry Review*. He has received an NEA Literature Translation Fellowship and numerous other awards.

You're Safe

Avital Gad-Cykman

Close your eyes, lean your head on me. The booms you hear are fireworks for the new year. It's not the new year? Fireworks from a nature party, then. This is what they are. There's a party not far away. The thumping bass sounds penetrate the walls. I'm holding you. Don't worry. I'm here. Maybe someone is watching a war movie. The booms are the TV's bass sounds. And fireworks. Don't cry. There's nothing to fear. The smell of burning? Not from our kitchen. I always make sure to keep everything safe. It's probably a bonfire. What do people sing around the bonfire? Let's sing together, very quietly, a song of the night.

Every night the breeze blows, every night the treetops hum, every night a star chants, blow the candle and sleep.

Your voice is so sweet when we sing in whispers. Let's repeat this lovely verse, forget the not so nice verses. They're just someone's fears, the poet's, but we aren't afraid, right? We must keep quiet now. The fireworks are very near, and the bonfire is big. We'll keep to ourselves and won't interrupt. No, nobody's shooting. I'm clutching the door handle with one hand. Stay close, I'll hold you with my other hand.

Avital Gad-Cykman is the author of *Light Reflection Over Blues* (Ravenna Press) and *Life In, Life Out* (Matter Press). Her work won awards such as Margaret Atwood Society Award and "Best of" anthologies such as W.W. Norton's Flash Fiction International, and appears in beloved magazines like *Iron Horse Literary Review*, *Prairie Schooner*, *Ambit*, and *McSweeney's Quarterly*.

Appetites

EMMA GOLDMAN-SHERMAN

After the divorce, my mother started to take me to this bar where she liked to order roast beef sandwiches "au jus." She said it meant bloody. I was 11 and horrified by the idea of blood, any mention of blood. The word lurched in me. She enjoyed herself and flashed a knowing smile as if she knew that soon blood would come pouring out of me. She released a glob of ketchup onto her pickles.

Your father never liked a tart pickle, she said. Your father never liked a decent meal.

She wanted me to dip my sandwich in the blood they served on the side like a thin gravy.

Dip it! She growled, drinking beer.

I wasn't dipping. I wasn't anything. I wanted to disappear, to be someone else, someone - according to her and everyone - I could never be.

She dipped her sandwich and shook it at me. See how the blood seeps into the roll? Kaiser rolls, she told me. Hard. Kaiser's German for king.

Blood hit the straw wrappers. I had a thing about squishing them down to the tiniest possible accordions. I used to be the official family straw wrapper remover. But it had been a while since we'd gone out as a family. They never agreed on where they wanted to go or what they wanted to do, and then, one day, his closet was empty.

The wrappers started to move, expanding like snakes. I added Mountain Dew from my straw to see how big they'd grow.

She stopped me, saying, you're making a mess.

I said, you started it.

She said, don't blame me for your life. Men are dicks. And she stuffed her mouth with the pink flesh and the soggy roll.

We got mine wrapped to go.

Emma Goldman-Sherman writes plays and poetry, teaches and works as a neuroaffirming coach. "Appetites" is the 3rd micro they've ever written. When they were 58, their first won 3rd prize in the *Fish Anthology 2023*. They support writers at www.bravespace.online and offer prompts at goldmansherman.substack.com

Anya Underground

RYAN GRIFFITH

It was *Penitent Magdalene*—tears in her eyes after washing the feet of Christ with her hair, breasts bared to God, both erotic and sorrowed—that Anya loved most, and now, crossing the square outside the Hermitage, wind grieving through the trees, she wonders how Titian captured the ecstasy of a woman abandoning everything—gold, clothes, herself— for a man-god, feasting on nothing but faith and desperation.

Soon she's at Sadovaya, her station, the city's teeth grinding down, down, underground, and when an intercom says *watch your step*, she stumbles off and sees her reflection in a train slide by like the face of a stranger in trouble, a person who might need her help, and then there's another train, and she boards with others heading to the end of the line, Kupchino or Veteranov, everyone zero-eyed, wheels screaming against steel. Across from her a woman's knuckles flex around a bag as if the bag itself is her salvation, and Anya's sight rises to a face much like hers, pale and tired but with an eye bruised purpleblack, memory-fresh, the reverb of bone still trembling into space, a throb she might call aubergine or violet but for the beauty of the words, the negation of pain by language. It reminds her that the ride must end, that soon she'll return to a battered room, a place where her husband is waiting, touching the red eye of his cigarette to the night, cognac blazing in his hand. The woman's face is bright in underground light and Anya stares at the pigment that will soon go green as bile, green as the silence of god, and for a moment their glances meet, and Anya watches the woman's irises dilate in recognition, black moons filling with her wound, thinking that perhaps this woman sees sad Magdalene crawling through the desert for her Christ, the holy brute who will redeem her. When the doors wheeze open they stand and bump shoulders, nimbused in mystery, and the woman's hand reaches into her bag and pulls out a plum, succulent and round, plump with darkness, and hands it to Anya, who nods, as if saying yes to question that only she can hear, and they both step from the train, anonymous, two women in the lifespans of their bruising.

Ryan Griffith's fiction has appeared in the *Wigleaf* Top 50 and *Best Microfiction*. He runs a multimedia narrative installation in San Diego called Relics of the Hypnotist War.

Mother Teaches Us to Play Tennis at Brookside Park

MARY GRIMM

Remember how the hill of trees rose up over the tennis courts like a dense green leafy wave, and we, my sister and I, tiny stick figures batting away at the ball, aware of our inadequacy in the face of mother's skill and expectations. She'd been a tomboy, as good as her brothers in everything or she'd know the reason why.

We dragged our sullen limbs through the hot air under the high early morning sun – couldn't we stay home and read a book? (No.) She was vital, thick like cream, robust, the swing of her racket a perfect curve we couldn't imitate.

When she was a girl she had come to these same courts down the railroad tracks from the zoo. She and her own sister, Eleanor, had held the courts against all comers, even the men. She told us this story in a happy reflective way and almost those ancient games began to take shape around us, the two of them in their old shorts and blouses darting around the court, the scores ringing out in tinny voices, 30-all,

40-30, 40-love, Eleanor jumping like a monkey on Monkey Island at the zoo and my mother smiling her secret smile, the sun shining on her blonde head, hair done up in a braid.

I hit the ball into the proper place, diagonally over the net, and for a minute it was as if I'd been inspirited by her younger self, feeling the strength of her arm, her unerring gaze, and maybe my sister felt it as well, poised on her toes and grinning. But when the ball came back my swing went wide.

We could hear the birds in the aviary cawing and hooting. It was time for lunch: cream cheese and jelly sandwiches, with chopped nuts for health, and a thermos of lemonade. Remember how she said you'll get better, and how we pretended to believe this, and almost did, so strong was the power of her faith in us.

Open the Door

MARY GRIMM

It was dark in the closet and it seemed as if they'd been in there a long time, so long that maybe their names had changed. Jeanie said this to Mark and he said don't be silly. Not said, but whispered, because of the glumps, which was what they called their grownups when they were "on the warpath," as their grandmother had once said. She was dead now. Jeanie didn't know what a warpath was but she thought it was a kind of drug because that made sense, right? It wasn't totally dark because they had a flashlight. It was dim because the battery was going. Its light was a dim greenish circle that Mark aimed at the walls, the clothes hanging on the rod over them, their feet. The light floated to glow on the ceiling and Jeanie imagined that it was a fairy who was their friend. Or maybe just her friend because sometimes Mark was mean about things like fairies. Was it time to come out yet? Mark said no. Whispered it. They were sitting on shoes. The dresses hung down smelling like dead flowers. My new name is Karla, Jeanie said. You don't look like a Karla, Mark whispered, so she rearranged her face to make it better.

Karla would be smart and a little taller. Karla would know when to open the door.

Mary Grimm has had three books published: *Left to Themselves*, *Transubstantiation*, and *Stealing Time*. Her stories have appeared in *The New Yorker*, *Mississippi Review*, *Helen*, *The Citron Review*, and *Tiferet Journal*, among others. Currently, she is working on a series of climate change novellas set in past and future Cleveland.

Luda, The Girl Who Was My Best Friend

STELLA FRIDMAN HAYES

Dressed in school uniforms, finely ironed by each of our mothers. Detachable starched stiff white Victorian collars around our necks. We would skip on a fresco of hopscotch. New concrete, erasing a small-town dirt road. We'd pick bright-colored chalk from a box of cardboard, our fingers covered in radioactive ash. How streaks of it end up on our faces, giving our nightly baths a painterly glow. Every day after school I'd go up to see her. I remember her a year or so older. A blond girl. I had more *pupsiki*, small rubbery Germanmade dolls — intricate, free. In their underwear & wardrobe of tiny dresses, sweaters, hats, shoes. We undressed & dressed them. Small choices in a country dispossessed of the *I*. In her home, voices were hushed, plans were made in daylight. When my parents confided in 9-year-old me the dangerous news that we were leaving, I couldn't tell her. We played, combed & rearranged each other's hair into monarchal braids. I wanted to leave my plastic friends for her but if I did, she would tell her parents. Maybe it started then, in Brovary, Ukraine, I liked blue eyes more than brown. Diaspora, my love

Stella Fridman Hayes is the author of *Father Elegies* and *One Strange Country* (What Books Press). She grew up in Brovary, Ukraine, and Los Angeles, and holds an M.F.A. in poetry from NYU. Her work appears in *Four Way Review*, *Poet Lore*, *Image Journal*. Previously with *Washington Square Review*, she's a contributing editor at *Tupelo Quarterly*. StellaHayes.com

A Memory of Dreams, A Dream of Memories

DAVID HENSON

One day the sun is so hot it evaporates our memories. They churn and mix in the clouds as we wander wondering what, who and when. After a few days, the memories rain to earth in random fragments. They flood city streets, gushing into storm sewers and out to rivers and seas to be devoured by fish. They soak the ground of fields, gardens and orchards, rising up stems, stalks and trunks.

When we eat, every bite releases a memory.

A man plucks a beefeater from his tomato plant. There's a burst of flavor, and a woman is running barefoot through a meadow. The memory is so vivid, he feels the dew and warm sunlight. But whose recollection is it?

A woman crunches into an apple. "I don't think this is mine," she says to a familiar-looking man. "A little boy pedaling a red tricycle and shouting *vrroom*. Is it yours?"

Another woman fights back tears after a taste of trout recalls an old man whispering to his failing black Lab.

Eventually everyone has a morsel of everyone's memories. Empathy glimmers among strangers. We laugh with borrowed joy, weep with shared sorrow. The lines between self and other blur like a water-color where ocean meets sky.

We admire the beauty and lose the memory of edges.

David Henson and his wife have lived in Belgium and Hong Kong over the years and now reside in Peoria, Illinois. His work has appeared in numerous publications including *Bright Flash Literary Journal*, *Ghost Parachute*, and *Literally Stories*. His website is http://writings217.wordpress.com and his Twitter is @annalou8

Vandals

SUZANNE HICKS

We enter the store with purpose, unassuming, heads down. We begin with the shampoo, drizzling honey-colored patterns on boxes of hair dye, filling the nooks around nail polish displays, but careful not to drip on the floor because we don't want to hurt anyone, just make a mess, maybe ruin someone's day. We grab handfuls from the bulk candy bins, stuffing our pockets, shoving some in our mouths, making chipmunk cheeks. We rush through the magazines and rip out pages with all the boys we love from movies and TV shows and bands and later cut out their faces to plaster onto the walls of our bedroom. We send each other signals when we're done, no one noticing our freshly wet *n* wild lip-glossed lips as we walk out the door. No one knowing we'll go back to a dark house where we search the kitchen, remembering forgotten birthdays when we find expired piecrusts at the back of the freezer that we eat smeared with chocolate sauce for dinner, imagining someday we'll learn how to bake them into warm pies filled with fresh fruit that we serve up in our bright houses.

Suzanne Hicks is a disabled writer living with multiple sclerosis. Her writing appears in *Gooseberry Pie*, *Bending Genres*, *Gone Lawn*, *Milk Candy Review*, *Maudlin House*, and others. Her stories have been selected for Best Microfiction and the *Wigleaf* Top 50 Longlist. Read more at suzannehickswrites.com

Motel Radio

LINDSAY HILL

My friend is like one of those motel radio alarm clocks that the person who had the room—before you had it—set and left and now it's going off in the middle of the night and you don't know what it is at first and you're struggling to find a way to turn it off and the song is loud and always something about a man who did his woman dirty wrong and wants her to take him back I would never take him back I would beat him to pulp with the handle of the payphone he's calling from I would beat him down in that phone booth I would break the glass with the back of his head I would break his ankles to bits in the collapsing metal door I would steal his car and wreck it and pull myself out of that wreckage and walk away and I would never take him back.

I walk the side streets littered and shining. I wander through overgrown gardens. I go to the ocean some evenings—one step—one step—one step along the shore. The somersaulting waters of the waves remind me how foreign a thing it is to be alive—how strange.

Lindsay Hill's work has appeared in *New England Review* and other journals. His first novel, *Sea of Hooks* (McPherson), won the PEN Center USA fiction award. His second novel, *Tidal Lock*, from which "Motel Radio" is excerpted, was published by McPherson in 2024. He lives in Los Angeles.

Mars

RICHARD HOLINGER

At dusk the crows crowd in, black clouds swarming to beeches stripped of leaves above a creek nearly drained by summer's heat. A pickup with a farmer and his son pulls up beside me. Some cattle got out of their pen, but, except for one lone calf still loose, the others followed the lowing home.

The radio reported this morning that in our lifetime Mars will never be so bright again. I wade through wild asparagus, spiny cucumber, and milkweed pods and with binoculars usually aimed at mud-grinding carp or slithery deer, look at the moon. Then move down, and right, the radio said. There.

* * *

A penlight probes my optic nerve. The doctor tells me retinas can detach in glaucoma eyes like mine. Why can't I be a Dylan Thomas raging at the night? Instead, I sit passively, fitted for new glasses, listening to lenses click clear, clearer, clearest, heavy on my nose.

* * *

A black box elder bug crawls over the first black

lines of a fountain pen poem. Deer loiter at the salt lick. The farmer calls to tell me the stray has not come home. He says if I see him to keep him close; he'll scare too easily to lead back home alone.

Through open windows I hear the cattle low, frightened at being penned. The birch sapling transplanted from Wisconsin spreads smoky branches up through the oak that ants are hollowing out, its bare, skeletal limbs entangling Mars, its life three minutes past.

Richard Holinger's work appears in *Hobart*, *Chautauqua*, *Chicago Quarterly Review*, and elsewhere, with several pieces nominated for a Pushcart Prize. Books include *North of Crivitz* (poetry) and *Kangaroo Rabbits and Galvanized Fences* (essays). A poetry chapbook *Down from the Sycamores* (Finishing Line Press) is forthcoming. He lives in rural Illinois.

Forecast

Vanessa Hua

After the weather turned, so did we. For many, the end of fog led to the end of patience. Though we'd heard the cool grey city might become sun-bleached as Seville by the end of the century, someday had arrived sooner than anyone predicted.

After the gloom failed to materialize in June, July, or August, a committee convened and proposed gene therapy. Like those tomatoes spliced with fish genes, we too might adapt. But funding evaporated like the fog we hadn't known defined us.

Like love, like bankruptcy, like sleep, the wild swings happened slowly, then all at once. Amid a gale, our brawling neighbors slammed into a eucalyptus that toppled and crushed them both. During a triple-digit, triple-week heat wave, teenagers tore apart my brother's classroom. Our grief deepened every time another ecosystem, another species blinked out here: the tiger salamander, the kangaroo rat, the marsh sandwort.

We survived largely on the belief that the fog's absence was an anomaly. Soon we'd return to those contrarian summers, the ones as cold as winter and the blankness upon which generations of us had projected our dreams. The clouds dropping down to swaddle but also to erase. We wished for silver—not the gold of this endless summer—but that of a fog bank pouring like cream.

It's been two years now, and, worldwide, fog is nearly extinct. The realization that my unborn child will consider it as they might a rotary phone or a Tesla leaves me unmoored.

As I wade into Ocean Beach—now merely bracing instead of heart-stopping—I ache for my firstborn, who will never dream about fog in the Avenues. Never call upon it as a metaphor, never curse the dampness that makes a home cozier upon return. Never turn porous in the mist with someone they love.

Their generation will come of age in a city where we've lost our taste for the temperate—our dispositions like palates scorched on too much sugar, salt, and fat. If only we hadn't been so self-serving, we might have forestalled disaster.

I halt before going too deep in the water, struck by the thought that the extreme is how we might find a way through. Not with seawalls or another stopgap, but an idea too outlandish for anywhere else, that might take root and flourish under every color of sky.

Vanessa Hua is the author of *A River of Stars*, *Deceit and Other Possibilities*, and *Forbidden City*. A National Endowment for the Arts Literature Fellow, she teaches at the Warren Wilson MFA and elsewhere. Previously, she was an award-winning columnist at the *San Francisco Chronicle*. Her novel, *El Nido*, is forthcoming.

Empty Nest

KATIE HUMPHRIES

While walking from our hotel to Caesar's Palace for a Sting concert last spring, we passed a child in distress. He was two blocks in front of us, zigzagging across the sidewalk in our direction. Pale, dirty face. Greasy, shaggy hair in need of a cut. He wore ripped, grimy jeans and a short-sleeved T-shirt that was once white but now gray. He couldn't have been more than thirteen. He moved like a rabid dog, swaying and lurching around the pathway, practically foaming at the mouth. It was the bare feet that got me. The boy stopped twice to kick at the sidewalk, oblivious to his vulnerable feet. Enraged and oblivious to the strangers around him. I looked down at my shoes, and blood rushed to my head. When I looked up, he was six feet away. But he did not see us. His eyes were fixed on something beyond, something that seemed to erase everything. After a few seconds, he swayed past us, our group of six empty nesters, dressed in sequins and luxury sneakers, out to enjoy a night of gin and tonics and live music. My girlfriend, Laurie, asked me about my youngest child's freshman year in college and whether his social anxiety had improved.

Just as I was about to answer, *He's better now*, the boy passed us by.

I am told Sting opened with "Roxanne" and ended with "Fields of Gold," but I don't recall much of the concert. What I do recall about that night is looking over my shoulder and watching the boy stumble away, his small, dirty feet leaving bloody prints that looked like bird feathers along the sidewalk.

Katie Humphries's stories have appeared in *NiftyLit*, *Grande Dame Literary*, *The Tomahawk Creek Review*, *Tahoma Literary Review*, and *Gold Man Review*. She has an MFA in Creative Writing from the Rainier Writing Workshop, an M.A.T. in English as a Second Language from Georgetown University, and a B.A. in English from Davidson College.

Spent

Ingrid Jendrzejewski

You go to pay for your groceries, and your credit card is declined. It was bound to happen sooner or later, but you didn't expect it to be today. You look at the letters dancing across the card reader's display and swallow.

The cashier doesn't blink an eye, doesn't look at you, just asks for another type of payment. Of course, you don't have any, but you make a show of rifling through your purse, wondering aloud what could be wrong. You feel a hotness radiating from your skin, a tremor in your throat. Still, you smile. "Probably something wrong with the chip and pin," says the cashier to her screen. "Happens all the time." The girl bags up your groceries, stows them in a cart off to the side so that you can go home and fetch your other card, the one you don't really have.

When you get to your car, you sink into the driver's seat, check how much gas is left in the tank, and then sit. You just sit. And as you watch other vehicles pull in and out of the spaces around you, you ask yourself exactly how long it takes for a pint of milk to turn.

Ingrid Jendrzejewski is a co-director of National Flash Fiction Day and an editor at *FlashFlood* and *The Prose Poem*. You can find her online at www.ingridj.com

Newlyweds

JONATHAN JOHNSON

The spring of his diagnosis they went out to the forest. In places cut before he bought the land, where the open sky bleached the ferns, they planted trees. Hundreds of trees. Each slender wand in their closed fingers. Each filigree of roots down into each damp hole they opened.

Engaged most of their middle ages in houses across town, they'd savored slow-waking alternate weekends together when their exes had custody. And once their separate sons were raised separately, as agreed, there'd been college financial aid implications to consider.

She'd finally moved into his house to recover from double knee replacements. She walked slow laps around the rooms downstairs—dining room office with the fireplace, archway to the living room where they'd moved the bed, archway to the entry, hall with the coat pegs, kitchen, back to the dining room office with the fireplace and fire he'd build her mornings before he left for campus.

Healed, she'd kept her place (where she lives again now) but more or less continued to reside at his.

Cards with friends. His crowds of books and papers. Her crowds of books and papers. Laptops opposite across the dining room table. Dusk clouds across the horizon at the beach two blocks away.

Sixteen years she wore an engagement ring.

Then the news.

Then the little wedding beside the little waves. His son's speech.

"Well, Dad finally found a way to marry Terry without making a long-term commitment."

Exactly his dad's humor. And one of my favorite jokes to this day.

Except, forgive me, it's not altogether true, is it? Even if they got a little less than two more months.

My other favorite joke?

Know why one side of a wedge of geese is longer than the other?

More geese on that side.

Every spring they come with their voices. Every spring they come sailing over those trees north of town for some wild lake beyond. Over those trees drinking and eating from the earth and breathing the sun.

"Newlyweds" is from The Little Lights of Town, **Jonathan Johnson's** collection of stories set in Marquette in Michigan's Upper Peninsula, forthcoming from Carnegie Mellon in 2025. His other books include two memoirs and four collections of poems. He teachers in the MFA at Eastern Washington University.

The Day I Went Missing

JESSICA KLIMESH

There were no gifts last year (or any previous year)—no tiered cake or pink champagne, no celebratory pomp at all—so this year I asked the mayor if the town might throw me a party, which he agreed to, even though, he pointed out, "It's rather self-serving, don't you think?" I admitted that it was, but what I couldn't even begin to explain was that, unlike him, I had once lived in a world where people had names, where yearly milestones were met with fanfare and hubbub.

The mayor eyed me curiously and then, after an unrestrained giggle, said, "It'll actually be delightful to have something to celebrate during the depressing month of January, with its snow-gray mist and vacant darkness, not to mention the commencement of another damn year to remind us how desperately fleeting time is," adding that he would organize a committee to decorate the streets and buildings with streamers and balloons of tangerine, turquoise, and red to really make the town pop with color.

A nameless reporter from a nameless newspaper interviewed me, wanting to know more about the strange upcoming shindig and, specifically, what my relationship with the mayor was—a worthless insinuation since, without a name, I was unidentifiable, rendering any gossip useless—and I explained to her that it was simply a celebration of the day, twenty years back, when I'd gone missing, just up and left my previous life and drove my Ford straight off the edge of the world, ending up in this quaint and peculiar alternate universe, in a place without a name and without cell service, both of which had immediately appealed to me. "But what was the catalyst?" the stunned reporter asked because, like the mayor, she also had no understanding of the kind of realm I'd left, so I recounted to her how people there were always competing to be the crème de la crème, to see their names beaming boldly on a marquee sign, and it all just became so tiresome that I decided to disappear, and now each year I celebrate that fortuitous day.

Naturally, the reporter never asked my name (why would she?), but it later occurred to me that, even if she had, it had been so long that I wouldn't have been able to tell her anyway.

Jessica Klimesh is a U.S.-based writer, writing coach, and editor whose work has appeared in *Flash Frog*, *Gone Lawn*, *Ghost Parachute*, *Cleaver*, *Gooseberry Pie*, and elsewhere. Her work has been nominated for the Pushcart Prize, Best Microfiction, Best Small Fictions, and Best of the Net. Learn more at jessicaklimesh.com

Mushrooms

KATHRYN KULPA

The baker's wife came running, her big breasts swinging like cabbages in a sack, and we laughed until we heard her shout, *They're killing everybody*, then we ran, too young for anything on us to swing, dust puffing up from the road, far-off sun shining weak and pale like milk strained through cheesecloth, everywhere pounding feet and shouting and somewhere, getting closer, sounds like breaking trees. Papa pulling his ax from the woodpile, Mama shooing the cows from the barn. *Run,* she said, *run to the woods, hide like mushrooms hide*, and we ran through twisty paths, past weary drooping trees, found deep piles of leaves, covered ourselves like we were already dead, soft earth receiving our bodies, we lay still as sleeping dead girls under leaf blankets and watched pinholes of light grow lighter, then dark again, smoke massing the sky, ashes forming shapes like when we used to watch clouds— *It's an elephant! It's a sea serpent!*—but these were the shapes of everyone we knew, our teacher, the doctor, the baker's wife, then Mama, last Papa, weaving dark shrouds to keep us safe, brushing us like soft hands before they blew away forever. We held hands, whispered their names, and that was how we said goodbye.

Settle

KATHRYN KULPA

Afterward, when you hold a cold washcloth to your face, he'll apologize. Apologize, like "You don't know how it was. You didn't grow up in a circus like that." *A circus like that*, and you picture his triple-bypass father, clown-nosed, still barking coarse jokes, his cowed mother, sneak-drinking. Sneak-drinking in the kitchen where you find her, looking for salt. Salt in the wound when she tells you if you could just have a baby it would help. Help him settle. Settle is what you did when you didn't know better. You didn't know better, you were young but felt old with dull hair and crooked teeth and the world was an envelope you barely dared to peek out of, but now you do. Now you do, and the car keys are in your purse, the Klonopin is in his drink, and when he asks if you forgive him you say yes. Yes, you say, and you don't know where you're going but you know it will be better. Better than a circus like this.

Kathryn Kulpa is the author of *For Every Tower, a Princess* (Porkbelly Press) and *A Map of Lost Places* (forthcoming from Gold Line Press). Her stories are published in *BULL*, *Flash Frog*, *Gooseberry Pie*, and *trampset*. She would stay up all night reading if you let her.

How to Become an Auctioneer

MATT LEIBEL

Practice talking like your voice is running a 100-meter dash against other voices and all the other voices can move their mouths faster than elite stenographers can type but you're confident that your voice is not only rapid-fire quick but is capable of enunciation that's clear as a bell, if bells could enunciate, the best bells in the business, and how much would you give to be the best in the business, how about ten, how about twenty, do I hear thirty, forty, fifty thousand, whatever it's going to take, you're going to give it, because auction-eering is in your blood, your daddy was an auctioneer and your daddy's daddy, and your daddy's daddy's daddy, going all the way back to five generations, do I hear ten, and you were sold on this long ago, there's nothing you'd rather do, the only problem is, do I hear there's a problem, the only problem is that you can't stop, the only problem is, everything is up for auction all the time, what do I hear for this pine tree in the park, this beautiful tree with flowering cones the size of softballs, let's start the bidding on this sunset, this picture-perfect sunset, deep red with orange and yellow streaks, a work of true passion by a benevolent God who makes art for art's sake, and how much for this attractive stranger, this beautiful person just passing by, what are they worth to you, not that we buy and sell other people, my God no, but what if we did, what would you be willing to bid, and even in your dreams you're selling paintings and pigs and plantains on the block and even broad, philosophical concepts like entropy or enlightenment for sums you can't believe, because there's always some bored hobbyist willing to hold up a stick, to shell out for the privilege of owning something, anything, there's always another item, and you wonder what it would be like to live a life where you're not constantly selling, where your mouth is not constantly moving, where everything would slow down and you could enjoy the silence in the air, the silence in your head, how much would you give for something like that, do I hear ninety, do I hear a hundred thousand, do I hear a million, do I hear

---

Matt Leibel's short fiction has appeared in *Post Road, Electric Literature, Portland Review, The Normal School, Quarterly West, Socrates on the Beach, Aquifer: The Florida Review Online, matchbook, Wigleaf,* and *Best Small Fictions*. Find him online at mattleibel.com

Of Ducks

RICHARD LEISE

All those ducks you've been feeding all summer?
The one you call Hillbilly because his beak is cracked
and deformed or something? So fun, so crazy how
he'd come up and rip the bag of bread from your hand
when you weren't looking. Well look at him now.
His leg is somehow all kinds of broken. Him unable
to fly and how he works hard just on his hobbling.

And your Grandma Pete who takes you to Argyle
Pond every single day knows it's wrong. To let an
animal suffer. So that's the only reason the two of
you brought the dog kennel to Argyle Pond and you
still don't know how but you figured out how to catch
him. That was the only reason why Hillbilly was in
Grandma Pete's bathtub. He was fed and safe and
not just from dogs but mostly from the other *ducks*,
ducks who attacked him and plucked his feathers just
for going for a wad of bread you threw his way just
for him. It wasn't a permanent type of situation. You
were going to let him go once he got better.

But all that your mom and dad and your aunts and
uncles talk about at the Family Meeting is the last

straw. That she has a wild ass duck in her bathtub. And who knows the diseases. And not even that, but how the hell it is that she wasn't even showering, anyway. Which you might think would be a point for team duck, but isn't.

The things about straws.

When your Aunt Gloria is drinking, when you're out for dinner at Applebee's, your mom counts the number of them. When it's Grandma Pete, and there's only one of them, she's a different sort of angry.

So they tell you they took Hillbilly to an animal sanctuary. And when you say Can we visit they say A duck? and laugh and this is on your way to Endwell Estates where Pete, who has nothing broken and eats just as easy as you could think is now being quite assisted as she goes on living.

Richard Leise writes and teaches outside Ithaca, NY. A Perry Morgan Fellow from Old Dominion University's MFA program and recipient of the David Scott Sutelan Memorial Scholarship, he published his debut novel *Being Dead* in fall 2023. His novel *Dying Man In Living Room* is forthcoming from ELJ Editions, 2026. He is @coy_harlingen on Twitter.

Baby on the Verge

JENNY M. LIU

Being fourteen is balancing on a bridge in the middle of the night and wondering if staying would bring just as much pain as going. You've already run away from home, hopped the brick wall out of the backyard and into the street, pounded the pavement in your white Authentic Vans and sweet little crop top, a half-broken iPhone stuck in your back pocket—the house key clutched between your sweaty knuckles like that's what'll protect you if someone decides you're sweet. You're out like you wanted. And you think it could turn into chaos in a second despite the fact it's dead out here, summer crickets and air con drone, suburban landscape—you silly goose, don't unravel now; but oh, here comes the urge, the longing to either call or confront your friend and ask them to run away with you. As if the tension of the house last Thursday could be forgotten, how it had been you and them and the dog, top 40 in the background, ten pages of a tabloid rag being crinkled beneath your knee. Their face so close to yours it drowned out the raised voices and scraping chairs roaring down in the kitchen. You can't stand the silence. You cook up this entire fantasy of them saying yes, of *really* doing this and gathering up the cash and stuffing your school bags with clothes, underwear, toothbrush and simply walking out of frame because you're tired of existing in these settings, and maybe leaving will just let those who matter *hear*. You teeter on the edge of having power if not for the destruction if you reach for it. You think it could be okay for a while leaning on another warm body, and you'll live on pie and coffee and Sunchips, and sacrifice everything to get on a Greyhound. But a car drives by thumping bass and wraps you in a cloak of cold sweat. It sends you scrambling into a pokey bush—you're so alert and your stomach is a pit and nothing outside is soft or safe. You grip your phone as the battery drains just from being on and admit your shame: the creature comforts will always call you to obey. You'll turn back and go home, using all the strength you've got to clamber back over the brick wall. Sore hands. You'll lock the back door as soon as your feet meet the carpet.

Jenny M. Liu is a writer and occasional poet from Nevada. Her work has appeared in *Waxwing*, *JAKE*, *Harpy Hybrid Review*, *Full Mood Mag*, and elsewhere. She has a website at jennymliu.carrd.co and is on social media @jennymliu

What I Can't See

MELANIE MAGGARD

Since they've turned the abandoned K-mart into a laser tag, there's nothing else that makes Margot happy. After our three boys are packed up and delivered to school, with carrot sticks they won't eat and apple slices that will brown in the cave of their lunch boxes, long after the edges of sandwiches are tossed in the trash, creamy cereal milk drying in puddles on the kitchen countertops, she'll be hiding behind wooden crates, heart pounding, sweat dripping down the middle of her shoulder blades where I used to kiss when we were new and fresh with each other. At night, with the lights off, she'll tell me how she dreams of laser light piercing her enemies as she jumps and flips and hides from everyone. She's a ghost in the room, someone to look out for. There's purpose to her evaporation into the shadows. While she's telling me her desires I drift off, her words weaving their way into my brain until I see the crisscrossing of laser beams against a backdrop of smoke, my wife sitting cross-legged on the floor with her arms outstretched to the sky, her body filling with a light so bright I can no longer look at her, it hurts too much. Then, one afternoon I come home and can't find her. I search the house, call her name, check her car in the drive, see her purse and coat hanging in the hall. She must be here. We boys must find her. We search for hours, peeking into closets and closed rooms, behind shower curtains and open doors, under beds and couches, until we find her, sitting at the kitchen table, tears streaming down her face as she tells us she'd been there all along.

Melanie Maggard is a flash and poetic prose writer who loves dribbles and drabbles. She has published in *Cotton Xenomorph*, *The Citron Review*, *The Mackinaw*, *Peatsmoke Journal*, *Emerge Literary Journal*, *X-R-A-Y Magazine*, *Ghost Parachute*, and others. She can be found online at www.melaniemaggard.com and @ WriterMMaggard

CDEFGA

J.W. McCollum

Dad accepts all offers: her beehives ($120), her boxing gloves ($10), her garden gnomes ($50), her wetsuit ($150), her welding hood ($30), her black Prada ($120). They carry it all away, past the sign in the yard, back to their big trucks and down the street to somewhere. The place Dad bought with Cheryl has a deck that looks on the beach. It has a bedroom and bathroom and an open area where they've stuck a fridge and a compact range. Downsize to upsize your life, he keeps saying, something he heard from his realtor.

The kids from the neighborhood joust her squash rackets ($25) down the driveway. They hobby horse her metal detector ($20) through the begonias and torture her mandolin ($40) in the garage. I had no idea she played the mandolin ($40) until Dad carried it down from the attic. Gorgeous. Rosy plumes erupting in the grain. Mother-of-pearl flames on the fretboard. She even wrote a few songs, he says, but Dad can't remember any. One kid croons Enter Sandman in an awful falsetto while the other head-bangs. Another string snaps.

I'll take the mandolin (~~$40~~), I tell Dad. In fact, I'll take it all. I can fit it: her crossbow (~~$80~~), her tiara (~~$100~~), her parachute (~~$75~~), her leotard (~~$100~~) her astrolabes (~~$200~~), her jazzercise tapes (~~$1~~), and all the other things that are hers and all the things that might have been but we can't remember.

My boyfriend says the apartment's become a sad museum. He stubs his toe on the dirt bike (~~$500~~) in my kitchen again, and now he's staying at his place. So I spend my nights in the wheelchair (~~$50~~) watching how-to-play videos on YouTube: C D E F G A. I hold the same strings she held, run fingertips across the same frets and wonder what songs she sang, hoping they'll find their way to me from somewhere. Some chords give me trouble, and my hand cramps after too long. It's only been a few weeks, but I'm making progress.

J.W. McCollum is from East Texas and writes emails and other things. His work has appeared in *Pithead Chapel*, *Flash Frog*, ScribesMICRO, and elsewhere.

Without You

KATHLEEN MCGOOKEY

After your wife dies, you write that you're moving back East, so I drive three hours to see you. You're dragging a hose across your yard, bandana around your head, not expecting me. *Let's sit by the river*, you say, and I ask, *Would you mind if I get my dog from the car?* Your hips give you some trouble with the stairs to the small wooden deck. We're talking about packing, selling the rare books, sedating your cat, when two chickadees land in the branches above your shoulder. They're waiting to eat from your hand. What will they do this winter without you? The sun warms our faces. While light sparkles on ripples the wind makes, you tell a story I've never heard: fifty-five years ago, you gave up a daughter, and now she has found you. You'd searched for her for years. I had no idea. *It's saved my life*, you say. At the edge of my vision, I'm aware yellow leaves are drifting to the water, I'm aware the river is carrying them away. My watch has slipped to the inside of my wrist; how long can I stay? My dog, who has slept between us all afternoon, sits up and yawns, and offers you his paw.

Kathleen McGookey has published five books and four chapbooks, most recently *Cloud Reports* (Celery City Chapbooks) and *Paper Sky* (Press 53). Her work has appeared in journals including *Copper Nickel*, *EPOCH*, *Glassworks*, *Hunger Mountain*, *The Los Angeles Review*, *North American Review*, and *The Southern Review*.

When She Falls

MARIE-LOUISE McGUINNESS

When you fell, your night was over. Stumbling was ok, you'd blame your shoes that were a little bit high and a touch too new, or a wayward pebble on the footpath. You'd smile at the bouncer and flick the flame red hair that made the boys go weak.

He'd scrunch his eyebrows and pretend to be unsure, tipping his head in imitation of thought, then he'd step backwards, allowing you to enter. We'd follow inside, relieved, loud music pulsing inside us, blooms of club steam clouding our faces.

But you fell.

And the bouncer knows falling means drunk, means tears, means vomit on chairs, in toilets and queues snaking from doors angry girls bang for admittance.

No, you're not getting in tonight, darling.

In an ideal world we'd leave with you, share the unmarked taxi with broken headlight, ask the driver what caused the black eye. We'd notice his gaze creep over your bottle-tanned thighs, slither up to your face of smudged make up, gears grinding in his skull, noting your melting wax features drifting to sleep.

Our skin would prickle as a lizard tongue stroked his chapped lips, tasting possibility, making a decision.

And we'd shout as he took the wrong turn down the unlit road of lonely houses, their window-eyes blind with nailed plywood. We'd threaten police and our fists as he switched off the ignition, and with our new salon nails, rip him to shreds as he lurched towards you.

But we'd spent too long preparing for the night out. We'd shaved our legs and applied pearly layers of slow drying lotion. We'd curled our hair with heated tongs, added extra strands from the plastic packet.

And Thursdays were hopping. Everyone we knew would be there.

So we went inside.

We didn't want to go home with you. We didn't fall.

Marie-Louise McGuinness has work in numerous literary magazines including *The Forge*, *Flash Frog*, *Fictive Dream*, *Milk Candy Review*, and *Banshee*. She has been twice nominated for the Pushcart Prize and longlisted for the Bath Short Story Award. She writes from a sensory perspective.

The Poet at Twilight

Joshua McKinney

He could not remember how it began. Perhaps it was his forgetfulness, the way he would read the same poem over and over and then exclaim, "I didn't see that coming!" Maybe it was because he had taken to staring out the window during storms, watching the rain weep down the pane and claiming he could read his name written in the wrinkling water. They told him he had done this, but he could not remember. Nor could he remember when his family had begun to conspire, but when his wife told him an agent had called inquiring about his new manuscript, he knew he had to play along. His daughter, whom he had begun to call Emily, found one of his poems on his desk, copied it, printed it, trimmed it to size, and pasted it in a copy of *The New Yorker*, which she left open on the coffee table. She even matched the font. His son, whom he addressed as Percy, or sometimes Gerard, handed him a twenty dollar bill and said, "Here, Dad, I cashed your royalty check for you." So frequent and inventive were their gestures that he found his vigor renewed. He could not remember when he had written with such zeal. He rose early to write, and he retired early to ensure he was rested. He needed rest because in addition to the long hours of writing, his wife had grown uncharacteristically amorous. If they happened to pass in the hallway, she would press herself against him and whisper, "Aren't you Mr. _____, the poet? I *love* your work." Each afternoon he would hear a soft knock at his study door, and she would enter, sometimes wearing some satin, slinky thing, but most days wearing nothing at all. And each evening when she called him to dinner he found the entire family seated at the table, and while they ate they asked him about his work, posing thoughtful questions about specific poems— which they had clearly read—and nodding intently at his answers. It was this act he appreciated most, knowing how difficult it must have been for them. He nearly wept at his good fortune. To be so loved!

Joshua McKinney's fifth book, *Sad Animal* (Gunpowder Press, 2024), was the recipient of the John Ridland Poetry Prize. His work has appeared in such journals as *Boulevard*, *Denver Quarterly*, *Kenyon Review*, *New American Writing*, and many others. He is co-editor of the online ecopoetics journal, *Clade Song*.

Separation

FRANKIE MCMILLAN

You can talk to the cow. Lay your cheek against her flank, position the bucket and, oh cow, you say, another blooming morning, another blooming day and you reach under the warm bulk of her, you grasp her full teats in your hands. You, ready, cow? Outside the trees stir, crankiness in the air, a flight of starlings over the barn. Soon the sun will light up the iron roof, blaze through the slats. Soon the calf will stop calling.

You can talk to the cow. About missing things. Your keys to the locked cupboard. Your boy. Where is he, you say, where did he go? The cow shifts in her stall. Her horns lightly toss the hay. Your feet grip the bucket tighter. Steady, cow. She turns her head. Blinks when you talk to her about missing things. Outside leaves gather, crisp as brown shirts. You talk about how the brown shirts scuttle across the field. How they mound up in piles, so deep a small boy can bury himself up to his neck. You can talk to the cow, even as her milk sprays out into the bucket. Even as it spills out over your wrist. The cow bellows. I know, cow, you say. I know.

Frankie McMillan is a poet and short fiction writer from Aotearoa New Zealand. Her latest book, *The Wandering Nature of Us Girls* (Canterbury University Press), was published in 2022.

Two Girls

SKYLER MELNICK

I am one of the girls. My sister is the other. Girlhood is something you do alone. We do it alone, together. There were never any adults. Not really.

My sister is paddling. She's younger but her arms are stronger, from all the whisking she does. Did. Before.

There is Before, and there is Now. Now is Boat. Our boat is on a lake so there aren't waves, but there are ripples. A bird will splash into the water to snatch a fish, or drown itself.

We are birds, my sister and I. We are two, yellow birds, escaped from our cages. We like to chirp instead of speak. Three chirps means I see land. Neither of us has chirped three times.

I chirp to my sister seven times. This means Stop Paddling It's Time To Relax and Talk About Life and Growing Up. We are only one year apart. Barely a year.

Are you hungry? I ask her.

Yes, she says. Are you?

Yes.

We are always hungry. We did not bring food. That is why you need adults. Adults have food. They also have tools, and can stitch you up if you crack yourself open.

The boat is cracked open. That is why I chirped seven times. It's going to sink, and paddling is wasted effort.

Do you see, I ask my sister, the hole in the boat? I considered not telling her, because I am the older sister, and that means I am almost her mother. But I tell her because girlhood is about unity.

What hole? she says, as water trickles into the boat.

My sister is good at denial. She is so good at denial that she didn't even flinch when Mother and Father fell off the boat. I pushed them, and that is how they fell. They do not know how to swim, and neither do we.

The water is rising, I say, as the water rises. Cold lake water, suckling our toes.

I don't feel anything, she says. She resumes paddling.

No, I say. Neither do I.

This must be what it means, she says, to grow up.

Yes, I say, as water rises to our waists. Growing up is feeling nothing.

I see land, she says, pointing. But she doesn't. There is no land. The earth is all water.

Skyler Melnick has an MFA in fiction from Columbia University. Her work appears in *HAD*, *The Pinch*, *Terrain*, and elsewhere, forthcoming in *Wigleaf* and *Fairy Tale Review*. She was awarded first place in *Fractured Lit*'s 2024 Ghosts, Fables, and Fairy Tales contest.

The Wives

DAWN MILLER

Sue is a drunk. Georgette is a flirt. Fiona wishes she'd never come to sports night, but here they are again, huddled in the kitchen playing Hearts while their husbands—buddies since college—whoop and holler over the football game on the large-screen TV in the living room. Sue slips into the mudroom at Georgette's house—it's her turn to host—and fills her glass from the mickey in her coat pocket. Her liver is fatty, and she'll die in seven years, but she thinks the news articles about zero alcohol being the only safe amount is a conspiracy fueled by tree-huggers and people who actually like yoga.

Georgette pretends she doesn't know what Sue is up to and rolls her eyes at Fiona. They get a strange enjoyment watching Sue implode, but they'd never admit it, not even to themselves. It makes them feel better about the extra pounds they each carry around their middle, and the cigarettes they sneak at night on their back porches when everyone's asleep, even though Fiona will be killed by a drunk driver in twenty years, the day after she quits smoking for good. When Sue's eyes and skin turn yellow, they'll drop off casseroles and send cute cards to placate their consciences with sayings like *Fuck Cancer* and *You've Got This!* and only sometimes wonder if they should've stepped in.

Fiona wishes she had better friends but finds it exhausting to keep up with lunch dates, birthday wishes, and Instagram posts. It's easier to hover along the edge of this little group stitched together by time, their husbands, and convenience. The truth is, Fiona doesn't like most women. She finds them petty and competitive. She'd rather sit with the men in the other room, but then she'd come off as stand-offish, and she's always prided herself on being polite.

Later, after the football game is over and yawns pepper conversation, the couples retreat to their own houses and unstitch the evening in minute detail. The women wonder—but never out loud—if this is all there is to their lives, if they've reached their true potential, or if their higher self spins somewhere out in the universe, one inch out of reach.

Dawn Miller's stories appear in *SmokeLong Quarterly*, *The Forge*, *The Cincinnati Review*, *Fractured Lit*, *Room Magazine*, and elsewhere. She is a 2024 *SmokeLong Quarterly* Emerging Writer Fellow and 2024 winner of the Toronto Star Short Story Contest. Learn more at www.dawnmillerwriter.com

River

CLAUDIA MONPERE

3:00 am and you need to pee but can't free yourself
from the sheets and blankets your legs move but you
can't figure out how to untangle yourself you're a fish
in a trawl net you're a mummy in linen bandages and
someone is wailing and you wish they'd shut up and
your husband turns on the light asking you to *calm
down please calm down* and you realize you're the
one wailing and your husband's thick hands tenderly
untangle you and he guides you to the bathroom and
the next morning you drink coffee and laugh about
it with the receptionist on the phone who says doctor
can't see you until next week and you agree it was
probably a night terror rare in adults but not unheard
of and your husband's in the background shaking his
head no, no–you must be seen today tomorrow at the
latest–but you confirm the appointment in a week
before he can grab your phone and hang up grateful
for the strong coffee and your sunny kitchen and you
will ruminate on this moment in your remaining
3.2 years which you understand is far longer than
the median survival of glioblastoma patients yet
you want to howl when people say what a gift it is

you want to gift them with malaria   smallpox
bubonic plague   and you disgust yourself with
this reaction which you confess to your two closest
friends who've taken you to the Russian River & who
say *you're fucking right* and *come on—now it's time to
swim* and they help you put on your bathing suit and
guide you to the river shore help you into an inner
tube and there you are the three of you drifting in
the river and the loud gigantic family in the cabins
near yours, the family with their barbeque family
reunion smells and water melon eating contests steers
toward you in their blow-up stadium islander eleven
of them crammed inside a beer in each hand and the
oldest woman leans out and gifts your friends and
you with beers but yours she opens and you feel her
wet fingers handing you the beer the sun warming
your shoulders dappling the river and you wiggle
your toes in the water and take a huge icy gulp and
you invite the day to bless you.

Claudia Monpere's flash appears in *Split Lip, SmokeLong Quarterly, CRAFT, trampset, Atlas and Alice*, and elsewhere. She won the 2024 New Flash Fiction Prize from *New Flash Fiction Review* and the 2024 Refractions: Genre Flash Fiction Prize from *Uncharted Magazine*. She appears in *Best Small Fictions 2024*.

Valuables

LYNN MUNDELL

Your uncle's wife is beautiful. Her face is soft and
unlined, like a pressed cotton handkerchief. Her hair
is brushed back in dark waves. Her laugh is small
and pretty, like a porcelain teacup when it touches
its saucer. She wears patterned satin scarves, heels,
pantsuits, gold pins she calls brooches on which the
animals' eyes are sapphires or diamonds. She drinks
milky coffee that she lets you sip while the other
women make Constant Comment tea. She has three
handsome sons. One day when you're a teenager she
surprises you by saying the rock star Peter Frampton
lives in the condo complex and likes to sunbathe with
her by the pool. Not long after, you stay for a few days
with her and your uncle. They never speak to one
another; the house is silent, like during a play when
the characters are waiting for someone unwelcome
to enter. When you learn to drive, your mother says
Aunt never did. When you go to college, your mother
the teacher says your aunt never went, nor did she
work. With time, you would think Aunt would lose
her luster, but you adore her even more when you
learn how her family married her very young to an

old man, who died. A fast marriage to his best friend, your uncle, followed. Much later the sons waste away slowly, painfully. Despite all this, Aunt is gracious, unruffled. In your 40s and now a wife and mother, you visit Aunt in her memory care facility, where she thinks you're her sister accompanying her on a cruise. The food is delicious. The waiters are sexy. The service is top drawer. She is what your own sister the nurse calls happy demented. When Aunt dies, you feel the same regret you do when something beautiful is broken, and part of that is the pain that she and so much more are in your past. Your mother calls you a month later. Aunt's closet is crowded with fur coats, like an entire forest of animals fleeing a fire. Her bureau is crammed with lingerie, at least 100 pairs of stockings. Piles of dresses, blouses, what your aunt called slacks, handbags. Everything so tasteful. Too small, too fancy for us. All wearing price tags, Mother tells you, while smothered in their own perfect wrappings.

Lynn Mundell is editor of *Centaur* and co-founder of *100 Word Story*. Her work has been published in *The Sun*, *Wigleaf*, *Tin House*, and a W.W. Norton anthology. Her chapbook *Let Our Bodies Be Returned to Us* was published by the University of South Carolina in 2022.

Laugh Track

WILL MUSGROVE

Your mom let me know there'd be televisions looping your favorite sitcoms, so I skipped the memorial. "A series finale," she called it. Imagine your relatives grieving in that church basement, hearing voices that remind them of you but aren't you. We watched a lot of TV, didn't we? I'd come over to your house after school because you had that comfortable sofa, and during the commercials, we'd switch off who was holding the rabbit ears. I know you want to know what I've been watching, but I don't turn on the TV anymore. I can't, not since I read online that most laugh tracks were recorded in the 1950s, that they edit in the sound after the fact, that most of those laughers are probably long dead. Maybe it's not true. Maybe studios can still find people willing to laugh, but I only hear you giggling. You're not there. You're stuck here, but I only hear you.

Will Musgrove is a writer and journalist from Northwest Iowa. He received an MFA from Minnesota State University, Mankato. His work has appeared or is forthcoming in *The Florida Review*, *Wigleaf*, *Pinch*, *The Cincinnati Review*, *The Forge Literary Magazine*, *Passages North*, *Tampa Review*, and elsewhere.

The End of the World Comes While You Are Singing Acapella in a Room Full of Strangers

CATHERINE OGSTON

Some people scramble up the stairs and spring out into the Sunday afternoon while you let your voice join the eight-part harmony and your feet make circuits around the concrete-floored basement. You hold the sheet music high and decide there isn't time to dwell on each of your regrets, although you allow yourself the brief hope that Sean will die alone. The ground trembles and the lights stutter; then you are walking in the dark while the choir soars. You let your paper float to the ground as a stranger clasps your arm, a last attempt to anchor themselves to someone else, and so you stand there singing to each other about love gone wrong. Suddenly you are thinking about the shy man, the one who smiled at you when he thought no one else was looking, from that summer by the lake and how for over twenty years you have had a lingering false memory that he wrote to you after you had flown home, because how could he have had your address and what did the letter even say. You feel the soft syllables of his name turning around and around in your head and wonder if he was the one that could have made you happy. The words of Good Luck Babe are still filling the room, almost loud enough to cover the noise of someone crying for a person that perhaps never even loved them back. You wonder how far the running people got and you allow yourself to hope that Sean's coworker is alone too. The song ends and restarts, all of you treading on the carpet of music, and as you sing you can almost feel the burning brilliant sun of that long-ago summer on your skin and the barely-there weight of that pale blue airmail envelope in your hand.

Catherine Ogston lives in Scotland and writes short and long fiction. Her work has been published in *New Writing Scotland*, *Bath Flash Fiction Award*, *Flash 500*, and *National Flash Fiction Day* anthologies and others, and has been long/short listed for the Caledonia Novel Award, Exeter Novel Prize, and Kelpies Prize.

I Have Lied To You

Pamela Painter

Before I leave my flat to meet you at six, at the Oak Room, where martinis arrive in tiny carafes on ice and the gin is surely Hendricks, I practice telling the mirror "I have lied to you." It is a confession long overdue. I remember how my lying eyes swerved away in the telltale sign you were too hurt to notice, but this time I promise myself I will not look away. Again, I lean into the mirror and say, "I have lied to you."

Oh, rouge, I forgot rouge, far more important than lipstick, so I pat it on my ashamed cheeks. Then as I whisper the third time, "I have lied to you," my hoop earrings suddenly seem far too dramatic. I set about exchanging them for—for yes, pearl studs—but a hoop catches in my long silk scarf, a sign, surely, that the color fuchsia is all wrong so I unwind it from around my neck and toss it on the bed.

This puts my charcoal sweater into stark relief, a bit too plain, so I pull it over my head, careful not to unravel the French braid you so admire. "I have lied to you," I tell my bare shoulders, realizing that if I'm to wear my ivory cashmere, I need to change my black bra for nude. Soon I am starting over in a nude lace bra, still admitting "I have lied to you." I cannot be later than usual, so I pull on my cashmere sweater, decide the black pencil skirt will do just fine, and lean in to tell the mirror one last time, "I have lied to you."

When will be the right time to tell you? Surely drinks will segue into a long dinner. Then into cozy nightcaps at your flat. And after that…..I turn from the mirror, gather up my purse and wrap. Really.

Really?

No. Better perchance to keep it to myself.

Pamela Painter is the award-winning author of five story collections. Her stories appear in numerous journals and anthologies, have been included in *Best Microfiction* and *Best Short Fictions*, and have received four Pushcart Prizes.

Screentime

ANGELINE SCHELLENBERG

Beside me on the sofa, my daughter is playing a video game. Only her eyes and fingers move. When I ask her how her day was, she doesn't answer. Or maybe my middle-aged ears have lost her frequency. On the screen, another version of her in a glittering lilac bodysuit is slaying skeletons and scaling cliffs. Set limits, they tell me. Keep trying to connect in the real world; she'll come around. I'm tired of picking my battles with a trained warrior. She has the controller, but I hold the remote. I press the up arrow. Beside me, her body flickers. On the screen, her bodysuit deepens to violet. I wave at the screen; she waves back. She looks so happy. I keep pressing up up up, until beside me on the sofa, the daughter I always wanted fades away.

Angeline Schellenberg is the author of *Tell Them It Was Mozart* (Brick, 2016), *Fields of Light and Stone* (UAP, 2020), and *Mondegreen Riffs* (At Bay, 2024). She serves as a contemplative spiritual director, second shooter for Anthony Mark Photography, and host of the Speaking Crow open mic in Winnipeg, Canada.

Outside

NINA SCHUYLER

And you would sit on the old bus seat we found on the corner near Quick N Easy, a stream of sunlight on one side of your face like a portrait. Sit and draw for hours in the nook of the apartment, and I would read, do the dishes and laundry, and take care of our baby. When I looked again, the sun was on your lap, your head still bowed as if in prayer.

I was outside this drawing. Outside in the garden, planting tomatoes and green beans, teaching our child about dirt and clouds and water. I remember her deep laugh like an old man when a squirrel ran right to her feet, perched on its back legs, and stared at her as if she were the most astonishing thing. Maybe she was a sound for you, maybe not even that.

Could we have done better? Could you have found me? Dare I say there were signs it was possible. In the glow of the beginning, you drew me, so many drawings staring straight at me, every contour of my face, the shape of my cheekbone, my ear, the little gap between my front teeth. I'd never been looked at so intensely, so carefully. But I wonder now did you ever really see me?

I can still see you all these years later, the sun pouring on you and the sheet of white paper, a blinding assault. When I gathered my things, the baby strapped to my back, you didn't even look up as I closed the door.

Nina Schuyler's short story collection, *In This Ravishing World*, won the W.S. Porter Prize and the Prism Prize for Climate Literature. Her novel, *Afterword*, won the 2024 PenCraft Book of the Year in Fiction and the Foreword INDIES Book of the Year Award for Science Fiction and Literary.

Forest Nuns in the Wild

ROBERT SCOTELLARO

I am raised by a band of forest nuns who have made their own way. Take refuge in hidden treehouses among the squirrels and woodpeckers. The Bible stories they tell are a mishmash of invention and tangled canon: the parable of The Boy Who Tickled Trees, and the story of Moses parting the field of red wildflowers... Sister Shrimp sometimes sleeps in the hollow of a great tree struck by lightning and Sister Much can lift large boulders over her head. We are kindly and pray over the small animals we eat, what we consider prayer. Our habits are made of leaves and we are all masters of camouflage and stillness, but the hunters rarely go this far in, and then we do not exist. God is the leaf, the soil, the moon, the worm... At night we drink juniper berry wine and play connect-the-dots with the stars and see things, fuss, of course, and even fight at times. Sister Shrimp is a biter. Afterwards, Sister Smart reminds us of the story of The Tree of Knowledge and how it was chopped down by a demented diamond merchant and used for mulch, and how we've been stupid ever since. The campfire we circle is a watchful eye gazing sideways in all directions and gazing skyward, and sometimes we look up too: sing sweetly to the heavens. Expect nothing in return.

Robert Scotellaro is the author of 9 flash fiction collections, and numerous poetry chapbooks. He has, with James Thomas, co-edited *New Micro* by W.W. Norton. His work has been included in two Norton anthologies, 5 *Best Small Fictions*, and 3 *Best Microfiction* award anthologies. Visit him at: www.robertsco-tellaro.com

Defpotec

PARTH SHAH

She's designing a new kind of contact lens. Lenses that melt. Every morning, the user inserts a fresh pair. They liquefy by night, coating the corneas in a refracting serum. Gradually the melting lenses bend the user's vision to 20/20.

She got the idea from her favorite nurse in the ward. He brings her oatmeal and fentanyl. He stays bedside until she's done, ignoring the arrhythmic chirping of his beeper. He's addicted to mouthwash strips. A hit to his tongue whenever she asks for a sip of water. The burn is healing, he explains, dropping an emerald tile into her mouth.

He believes in her invention even though she's dying. He always asks to see her new sketches, her new notes. Handwritten. Faint.

She's a sophomore majoring in architecture. But she tells him she comes from a family of ophthalmologists. Her last name, Snellen, comes from Herman Snellen, creator of the eye chart:

E

F P

T O Z

The first three lines are tattooed on her right tricep. A ceremonial mark to remember the third Friday in March, when her older sister matched into her top residency.

He wheeled her older sister out of this room the day after they arrived, crushed and ruddy from the car wreck.

She says, my sister had the next five lines tattooed on the back of her left arm:

L P E D

P E C F D

E D F C Z P

F E L O P Z D

D E F P O T E C

She says, when I get back to school I'm gonna take an entrepreneurship class.

The prescription name for the lenses is gonna be Defpotec.

Defpotec means 20/20, that's what the commercials will say.

Can you look up and see if a drug with that name already exists?

He pacifies her with a mouthwash strip.

What if my idea dies with me?

Your idea will live.

When ideas are born, there's no umbilical cord. Your idea is a kind of fire.

He touches his tongue.

But ideas don't burn. Ideas dissolve.

Parth Shah lives in Mexico City, where he tries to draw and write daily. His work also appears in the *Best Microfiction 2023* anthology.

The Incident

CHERYL SNELL

after In the Clouds by Jacek Malczewski
(Poland) c. 1894

Those kids were asking for it, who told them to
joyride the tractor like that— slamming on the brakes
for a bird whiffling through the air like some cork-
screw opening dreams that they (like everyone) had
of flying, knowing they would surely fly someday but
never thinking it would be that day, the dust cloud
rising, harsh braking lifting them out of their seats,
tire tracks furrowing the field where grass won't grow,
not to this day, especially not on the spot where, if
you view it from a distance, it looks for all the world
like angel wings opening.

Cheryl Snell's books include fiction of all sizes and poetry. Her
work has been included in anthologies including a Sundress
Best of the Net, and most recently her words have appeared in
Blue Unicorn, *The Dribble Drabble Review*, *Switch*, and *Does It
Have Pockets?*

Our First Night Together

CHELSEA STICKLE

My lover presses his thumbs against the spine of a snap pea until it splits so he can fish out the peas inside. His mammoth hands, the ones that have completed surgeries, are operating at my table. *Crack, crack, crack.* "This is how we eat them at home." His eyes widen. "I once ate ten pounds in one sitting." I laugh and imagine the size of that pile, the number of bowls involved. With him, I'm trying new things. I'm living more in the moment, so I mirror his movements. The peas are sweeter than any vegetable has a right to be. This is his world: sweetness that comes from the earth. I only get sweetness when I mix ingredients. "Except they're bigger inside. Sugar peas? Sweet peas?" "Sweet peas," I answer, remembering the Bath & Body Works label of my youth, and pop more into my mouth. They're sweet, sure, but I like the way the pods mediate the flavor. It's more complex. *Crack, crack, crack.* He's not interested in the pods, and all I can think about is waste. Without his mouth or hands on me, I'm working equations to see how we fit. He distracts me with another story about home. I bite into an empty pod. A little boring without the peas but still a solid, stand-up flavor. Pure chlorophyll. Better together, though. Nature in its wisdom pairing them. The sweet and the solid. *Crack, crack, crack.* The pods pile up on my lover's plate. He offers to feed them to my bunny. Disappear them inside him. I say "maybe later" when I mean "no" because "no" would involve explanations he doesn't actually care about. What he wants is for me to finish eating so we can go back to what we were doing before both our stomachs grumbled in protest until they were a soundtrack we couldn't ignore. But I'm not sure what I want, so I grab another empty pod and bite down. *Snap.*

Chelsea Stickle is the author of the flash fiction chapbooks *Everything's Changing* (Thirty West Publishing House, 2023) and *Breaking Points* (Black Lawrence Press, 2021). She lives in Annapolis, MD, with her black rabbit George. Read more at chelseastickle.com

Tikbalang

CHARISSE J. TUBIANOSA

Mama likes to tell me that, when it rains but the sun still shines, a tikbalang—a fearsome beast, half-man, half-horse; that trickster—is getting married.

She tells me this because she married one.

He's not all bad, Mama likes to say about father. Nor all that good.

I look away, outside, at a cloudless night sky. The floorboards tremble, groaning under the storm of his hooves. My hands fly to my ears. In the morning, I see he's taken a chunk out of Mama's face.

Still, she makes him coffee; he kisses her where her mouth used to be.

Charisse J. Tubianosa is a Filipina-Spanish writer based in Barcelona. Shortlisted for the 2024 First Pages Prize and a flash fiction finalist for the 2022 London Independent Stories, her stories appear in *Spanglish voces*, *Sunspot Lit*, and *The Offing*. She is an alumna of VONA and the Tin House summer workshops.

The girl goes

Cathy Ulrich

with the wrong man to the wrong place;

with the right man in the wrong car;

with the wrong man in the right car, the windows down and that song on the radio that sounds like *freedom*, the fingers of her right hand tipping out into the wind;

across the street without looking;

into the mouths of our mothers and their *don't go there alones*, the ever-lengthening hems of our dresses;

out too late at night under flickering streetlights, her keys in her hand the way she's been shown;

to that part of town good girls shouldn't go;

to the bar alone, heavy cocktail glass in her hand, fallen laughter on her lips, smiling at the right men, the wrong men, drinking until the stool teeters;

out in heels too high, stumbling on sidewalk dips;

too close to the road, too far from the shoulder, into the glare of flaring headlights;

out of this story and into all of our stories, not our brothers' and fathers' stories: girls' stories, warnings and whispers, scoldings and bewares, and there she stays and there she shines, like a flaming, fallen star.

Cathy Ulrich is the founding editor of *Milk Candy Review*. She lives in Montana with a cat who is not as small as you have been led to believe. Her work has been published in various journals and anthologies.

The Meaning of Words Unknown to Doug

KAREN WALKER

- *matutinal: occurring in the morning*

  Doug is not at the kitchen table with his oatmeal. He's in the garage under the Chevy, stuck in a pool of thick oil.

- *jentacular: pertaining to breakfast*

  Louise stirs *You could've died* in a pot on the stove. Pours it into her bowl and his. Despite a kiss on the cheek and an extra spoonful of brown sugar, Doug denies needing anyone's help or ever wanting oatmeal.

- *dès vu: the knowledge that something has become a memory*

  As the dealership changes the Chevy's oil, Doug sinks deeper and deeper into a leather tub chair in the customer lounge. There's only complimentary latte. No coffee. What's a latte?

- *acatalepsy: the impossibility of comprehending the universe*

  At least six—!—building permits would be required

to convert the spidery garage into a den or other living space.

- *umarell: a retired individual who stands and watches construction sites*

When the strip mall was finished, the guys signed a 2x4 and presented it to Doug. They gave him leftover insulation and wire, promised to come see his garage renovations. They haven't, and he hasn't applied for a single permit.

- *catastrophize*

When Louise's preliminary results come back, Doug paces the garage. It's thirteen of his Please-God-save-her-I-can't-be-alone shuffle steps wide and twenty-five long.

- *saudade: a longing that's as hazy as it is powerful*

He grew up a grease monkey in his father's garage. Mechanics taught him how to change a Chevy's oil. Doug recalls them slapping his back, tousling his hair, shouting, *Attaboy!* and maybe even, *Proud of ya!* Doug's father, being forever busy with oil changes, did not.

Karen Walker (she/her) writes short in a low basement in Ontario, Canada. Her most recent work is in or forthcoming in *New Flash Fiction Review*, *Exist Otherwise*, *antonym*, *Ark Review*, *Misery Tourism*, and *Does it Have Pockets*.

Christmas Markets, Strasbourg, France

S H E R E E   W I N S L O W

Visiting Christmas Markets in eastern France was part of a final effort to save your relationship with your Parisian fiancé—a trip scheduled to ensure he didn't spend time with his no-longer-hidden other lovers or some unsuspecting tourist he seduced at the Louvre the same way he snared you. But by the time you strolled through lots of wooden kiosks inhaling the smell of sweet Glühwein while inspecting crystal snowflakes hung from red ribbons or ball ornaments painted with landscapes of snow-covered trees and frozen lakes, he knew you knew. Your hurt, his anger at being found out—it was a toss-up which of your emotions would cast the bigger shadow on any given day. The last night in Strasbourg, he raged, insulted you, called *you* the stupid slut. All night long, you tossed and turned, knowing he wasn't worth the abuse, thinking of ways to leave. You'd have to arrange a ride back to Paris but you had keys to the apartment, could swing by for the rest of your luggage before heading to the airport. Instead, when you got up at 6am and he criticized your cold shoulder, you told him he'd need to treat you better if he wanted a friendly morning greeting. All these tainted memories rush forward nearly seven years later when you're in the shower applying Peace Rose Oil hair conditioner to your head. Somehow the description on a tube of product plucked from the clearance section of a discount store is all it takes to remember those days of no peace. A few days earlier, a gunman had killed four in Strasbourg at the Christmas Markets so your mind was mulling the surprise of viciousness in places constructed for joy. You rinse under a stream of hot water wringing these thoughts together, grateful that you weren't shot when you visited, but also knowing bad memories should not be diminished by such low expectations. *Expect more*, you tell yourself. *Expect more*.

Sheree Winslow is deeply curious about the world and its people. Her micro essays about location have appeared in *Brevity*, *The Master's Review*, *River Teeth*'s "Beautiful Things," *Passages North*, **82 Review*, *Wanderlust*, *Midway Journal*, and *Storm Cellar*, among others. Sheree received her MFA from Vermont College of Fine Arts.

Where Did You Go?

FRANCINE WITTE

I went thin as pears, all sliced-up and see-through. I went halfway to happy. I went to a place where I don't have to answer. I went sniff in the air. I went to the arms of another. I went bent as bones. I went to a job without a computer. Where I stand in a field and the sun wets my back. I went behind the numbers on a wristwatch. I went hundreds of miles from your eyes. I went all unmarriage and you cannot stop me. I went where your questions stop smack in the air and long before they can get to my ears. I went to before I even know you. That spot in the morning about to begin, that curl of a mouth turning into a smile, that moment a flower opens up like a hand.

Francine Witte's stories have appeared in *SmokeLong*, *Wigleaf*, and many other journals. They have been anthologized in *Best Microfiction*, *Best Small Fictions*, *New Micro*, and *Flash Fiction America*. She lives in NYC.

Fish Soup

JENNY WONG

When auntie makes fish soup, the fish she uses is mostly whole. Scales are scratched away. Slippery innards are untwisted from the body. Only flesh, fin, and bone are kept. When the soup is ready to serve, she will say who each bowl is for. I am given the one with the least bones. Auntie knows that the fish from my childhood were mostly fleshy bits breaded into sticks or compacted into the roundness of a can. I never learned to watch what I chewed. Though she does her best, she cannot remove all the bones. Even this is a lesson that shows her heart. She teaches me that not all things are safe, no matter where we are. Eating this soup takes work. Awareness. Careful teeth. A cautious tongue. Tomatoes, potatoes, broth, flesh. Mind what lies among the comfort of soft things. My teeth search for the sharpness of tapered shapes, while my tongue fumbles with removal. On my plate, a pile of small successes. The men at the table complain and grumble around their chunks of fish, while my auntie has taken all the complicated bits—skull, fins, tail—skillfully discarded without a sound, displayed by her bowl, cleaned of skin. A silent monument to everything she does, and to the secrets only her mouth knows.

Jenny Wong is a writer, traveler, and occasional business analyst. Her favorite places to wander are Tokyo alleys, Singapore hawker centers, and Parisian cemeteries. *Shiftings & Other Coordinates of Disorder* is her debut chapbook (Pinhole Poetry, 2024). She resides in Canada near the Rocky Mountains.

Woolworth

DIDI WOOD

You won't remember me, an unfamiliar, under-sized, unkempt child of five clutching your coat in Woolworth. Why would you? It was so many years ago and it was nothing, nothing happened or so my mom said. We were walking, walking fast, my mom my little brother my little sisters me, the baby already fussing so no time to linger by the toys, although my steps slowed as we passed, eyes gulping all I could before it was gone. There was the Barbie I asked for but Santa forgot; there was a tutu like Christine Vickers had because she did ballet but we had no time for ballet, my mom said, no money, the wrong hair, we were not ballet people. And then we were in vacuums and I looked up and said *Maybe next year Santa will* – and the woman whose coat I grasped wasn't my mom, she was prettier than my mom, shinier, gleaming curls and a ruby mouth, her coat so soft and her perfume, oh, sometimes all these years later that scent wafts by me in a store, on the street, and I pirouette back to that moment, my grubby hand clutching your coat and you smiling, allowing it, a brief tranquil interlude we spent just considering one another before my mom bustled up, scolding, my siblings a roiling moat around her, and I started to cry and you said *Everything's fine now* and even your voice was velvet and my mom bundled us all away but it wasn't fine, I wasn't fine, I would have gone with you, resplendent in the shimmer of your scent, your smile, I would have been your ballet girl or your Barbie doll or anything at all, anything, anything, I wouldn't have looked back.

Didi Wood's stories appear in *SmokeLong Quarterly*, *Okay Donkey*, *Ghost Parachute*, *Fractured Lit*, and elsewhere. Her work has been selected for the *Wigleaf* Top 50 and nominated for Best of the Net and Best Small Fictions. More at didiwood.com

Invisible Roads

JANAYA YOUNG

There is a road just outside of town, east about ten minutes, that only goes down, both ways. If that doesn't suit your fancy, you could head west out of town where there is a road that curves so much you think you must be driving in circles but at any point along the way if you stop and get out, everything you see will be new, in every direction. We also have a road that always puts the sun in your eyes and another where you are guaranteed to break down. We tried to put an auto shop out on that road but the tow trucks kept breaking down. We've wondered which came first to the desert, these roads or our town. It was puzzling how none of us could remember, not even the oldest. Though, I think the roads have always existed, plodded by stray goats and coyote long before we came here.

Of all the roads, my favorite cuts right through the middle of town, and no matter how you walk, it takes you to a stream babbling away. On its muddy banks grow the most gorgeous of grasses, thick and tall, and on the other side of the stream is the meadow where we bury all our dead.

Janaya Young currently writes from Boston where she lives with her husband and daughter, though her writing will forever find its home in the Rocky Mountains. She has an MFA in Creative Writing from BYU. Her short fiction has most recently been published in *matchbook*, *365tomorrows*, and *Segullah*.

Manual for an American Novice in a Small Indian Town

TARA ISABEL ZAMBRANO

Bring a large crate of bottled water, a hand sanitizer, and toilet tissue rolls. Fold your hands in Namaste only when you come in or are leaving. Convert the locals with your sunscreen and lip balm, your style of adjusting the shades on your eyes, the way you mouth *Hello*. Say you love the saffron painted (triangular stone) Lord Hanuman under the hundred-year-old banyan. According to mythology, the tree is a home to shapeshifters—if you are (un)lucky, one may fall hard for you and follow you around for the rest of your sweet life. Inside the dim-lit room, unpack your things and look in the old mirror. Shake off (your privilege) clothes before wearing them—sometimes lizards will fill themselves inside your shorts and t-shirt, sniffing, licking where your skin was. Eat warm khichdi only. Don't fret if you are unable to sleep because it's monsoon and the stray dogs are barking crazy, howling, and frogs are making sounds (like your neighbor in the old apartment building in

NJ). Wear slippers or shoes at all times. Treat your throat infection with prayers and an abundance of chai. Watch the rain hanging in the air for days, then the unruly heat flattening your eyelids. In the roadside bazaar, roam around until your skin is translucent. Get over your lust for your half-Indian half-British college roommate by flirting with the woman who sells accessories and miracles. Take a census of the tattoos on her feet and arms, marvel at her clay-brown irises, her concave belly after four kids (possibly three daughters followed by a son). Procure bindis, glass bangles, and witchcraft to fend off men who snatch purses and jewelry, pick pockets. Under the streetlamp with moths swirling around it like a tornado, smoke beedis with her, and feel the tobacco scratch your skin from the inside—that itch of knowing more about the world. Ask the guest house attendant where you can get Indian beer, your fingers softly tapping and curling on the counter. Drink it for breakfast. Clean the dirt under your fingernails, don't shave your legs or armpits for the full experience. Before you leave, watch the humidity outdo itself. Pack your things, look in the mirror in your room. Put your hand on your chest and feel the fluttering wings of the moth you accidentally swallowed.

Once in our home in Agra, the monsoon was over

TARA ISABEL ZAMBRANO

and there was no water or power for a day so we waited forever—our mouths lusting to speak half-truths about making out and going braless in the back seats of the cars and when that could not distract us, we ran to the open terrace, sucking lollipops and since there wasn't a soul outside in the heat, we took off our PJs, and became the afternoon—our earlobes and neck, our limbs and nails turning pink from the syringe of the sun, asphalt gritting our feet, downstairs our mothers calling our names circled red with curses <slurp> we stuck our technicolor tongues out in the direction of the Taj Mahal that made everyone believe that men could become immortal by mourning their young wives, and call it devotion—well, no one had ever been more intimate with us than the tangerine light that flushed and freckled our faces and rubbed stars on our backs every night—so yeah, in the ocean of heat—white as the mausoleum's marble—we shimmered like mermaids, moving haphazardly as if our bodies would break free and never, never be like our mothers' when they slept next to our fathers, cold and lonesome, their hands folded on their bellies, yearning to feel something other than their skin holding the promise of unattainable forever—like queens in their dark graves.

Tara Isabel Zambrano is a South Asian writer and the author of a short story collection *Ruined a Little When We Are Born* from Dzanc Books. She lives in Texas. More at taraisabelzambrano.com

Holothurian

ADDISON ZELLER

At the cove, my father explained holothurians to me: the sea cucumber.

He had been quiet all day, but he was excited now that he had seen one on a rock just under the surface. We looked down into the clear water at the holothurian. It had dots on its cylindrical body like eyes on a moth's wing. I did not want it to be alive.

"The hole there is an anus. This animal is essentially a living colon. Life in its simplest form. Basically just a digestive tract."

A small face peered out of the holothurian's anus.

"Pearlfish like to hide in it."

When I leaned over to see the pearl fish clearly, I put my foot close to the holothurian.

"Better not," he said. "Stressed or threatened, it self-eviscerates."

But white thin tubes were already sliding out of the anus like spaghetti from a pasta maker. The startled fish shot past my ankles.

"Of course," he said, wearily.

The holothurian deflated into a small, leathery brown pouch.

"Dead?" I asked.

"No, no. Just very tired."

So was he. I could hear it in him. The day was over now. He took us back home and sat quietly until it was time to go to bed. When I got up in the night, he was still sitting there.

My father was interested in everything. He had an encyclopedia in which good and bad angels were listed and described. There were six hundred entries. I believe I read an entry for an angel—good or bad I don't remember—that was known to self-eviscerate from a hole in its head: a mouth or an anus.

Another angel was made entirely of eyes.

Some were wings, some were cylinders.

"You understand I can't take it anymore? That it's too much?" he would ask.

I would shake my head, or pretend I didn't. But he made it impossible to say nothing. Once, I nodded yes, it was too much.

That was all he needed: a person to say so. He began to deflate.

I can't find the entry about the angel. I once saw a holothurian dried in a jar.

Addison Zeller's fiction appears in *3:AM*, *The Cincinnati Review*, *minor literature[s]*, *LIGEIA*, *hex*, *ergot.*, and many other publications. He is a fiction editor for *The Dodge* and lives in Wooster, Ohio.

Three Hearts to Love Myself

ELENA ZHANG

When the ice age strikes, I grow an extra limb, then two, then three. They spring from my body, rows of suckers popping up along their muscular length, wiggling in the air like newborn tongues. My husband stands there in the kitchen and shouts at me, his face turning coral pink, *goddammit Beth you stop this nonsense right now*, but his words freeze in mid-air, his grubby, creaking fingers snatching fruitlessly at my powerful swirling tentacles. By then, I am already slipping out the door, my new limbs slapping wetly on the pavement, and the last I see of him through the window is his gaping fish mouth as his eyes burst open with ice crystals. Down down down I surge into the ocean, escaping sub-zero temperatures, escaping oxygen, shooting water through the holes in my body like a rocket as I gurgle out salt bubble laughter. I am classified as a dumbo octopus, I can fly, I can fly, I'm soaring. The colder it gets, the faster I propulse. In the dark, I become gelatinous, the purple bruises dotting my skin now just a part of my shimmering chromatophore camouflage, and I live there in the abyss for thousands of years, because down in the midnight zone, you can be soft-bodied and still be a predator.

Elena Zhang is a Chinese American writer and mother living in Chicago. Her work can be found in *HAD*, *The Citron Review*, and *Lost Balloon*, among other publications. She is a Pushcart Prize and Best of the Net nominee and was selected for Best Microfiction 2024.

ESSAYS & INSIGHTS

Architecture of Truth

Tara Isabel Zambrano

Decades ago, during the summer I visited Agra to see the Taj and afterwards arrived at my husband's ancestral home amidst a scheduled power cut. All the ladies in the house were covered from top to bottom, sweating profusely, and serving us chilled sherbet and refreshments without a sign of exhaustion or irritation on their faces. It made me want to say something, but I didn't because I was new to the family, I was new to marriage. I was new to tradition and new to finding my voice. A picture of Taj Mahal I saw online brought it all back and the story "Once in our home in Agra, the monsoon was over", unfolded. The tenderness of youth sealed with the mortar of expectations. The cold darkness of death and patriarchy. It took me several weeks to write it. I was coming out of a hibernation of not writing since the summer of the previous year. The words were difficult to find.

Months later, I wrote, "Manual for an American novice in a small Indian town" infused with facts, myth and history. I wrote it in one go. I hoped to find intrigue in what looks like an uncomplicated, simple living from the eyes of a tourist who's in search of magic. After all, what is a full experience whether it's looking at the Taj Mahal or living temporarily in a town with limited means?

To me it's seeing things as they are.

Since I started writing, I have studied my work to understand myself. What are my underlying issues? What do I return to? Am I able to convey facts as they are?

Here both pieces intersect in terms of privilege, internal and external conflicts, atmosphere of heat and simmering monsoon. They are two ends of the same thread. The thread of identity and discovery. The thread of wanting to know. I unspool it at every chance I get. I tug at it; I keep it taut. It's the heartbeat of my work. It's all that matters.

Craft Essays

Mary Grimm

Mother Teaches Us How to Play Tennis at Brookside Park

This is one of a series. I think of it as the mother series, where I try over and over to imagine and re-imagine my mother, sometimes close to her (our) real life, sometimes in more fanciful and farfetched situations. She was the sort of woman who seems to be all on the surface, cheerful and open, but this was deceptive. She kept things hidden even as she spoke about them. My sister and I were enraptured by the story of her childhood on a farm, told to us in a series of funny stories. It was only when we were adults that we realized those stories were like fairy tales, the kind where something ugly and frightening is prettied up or made humorous. In this story the mother is engaged in another sort of myth making – trying to give her daughters something, but also to make and remake them, in the image of herself, but better.

Open the Door

I often write rather autobiographically, but Jeanie and Mark come from somewhere else, from the darker places in my imagination. I haven't been in their closet, but I know people who have, who have hidden in the dark, who have tried to live by a set of rules they barely understood, who are still carrying the weight of that into their adult lives. I've wanted, sometimes, when the only thing I could do was listen, to be able to go back in time and open the door they hid behind. This story and those like it are the closest I can come.

Stories We Must Tell

CHRISTINE H. CHEN

James Baldwin once wrote that "Every writer has only one story to tell...," which describes perfectly how I feel about "Where Is Home?" There are experiences in our childhood that are so moving and formative they reverberate throughout our adult life often and with such intensity that we must tell them repeatedly. "Where Is Home?" is a question I've been asking all my life, having traversed continents and languages as a child of the Chinese diaspora before settling in the US. When I think of home, I remember fragments that collide and collate into one large tapestry: aroma and the taste of *char siu pao* I used to eat as a child living in Hong Kong, the sound and feel of the breeze among palm trees in Madagascar, the enveloping fog in San Francisco when I first arrived in the US—pieces of an immense puzzle to be filled in. "Where Is Home?" is a narrative of this fragmentation, uprooted life, a search for identity, themes that continue to creep into the prose I write in various forms, but which remain, at their core, the same story asking the same question: where do I belong?

"Mary" came to me after I noticed statuettes of the Virgin Mary inside arched niches in the yards of the houses I visited when I moved to Boston, MA, from Pittsburgh, PA. I later found out they were also "backyard shrines," symbols of a cultural and religious identity that owners of the homes treasured. Being brought up by staunchly atheist parents, I imagined how a non-Catholic mother like mine would have reacted, but I also thought of how in the culture she and I grew up in, we worship our ancestors; we place bowls of peaches and plates of steamed chicken in front of our ancestral altar, we splash wine on the floor to signify drink offerings, we light incense and bow in front of tablets inscribed with the names of our ancestors. How do we, as a society, become humbled and accept those who do not worship the same way we do, those who look different than us, who do not share the same beliefs? Can I, as an author, tell a story to help a reader shift from a hardened stance to acceptance like Ah Ma in that story? I hope so.

Five Questions for Lynn Mundell

WITH KATHRYN KULPA

My introduction to your work was the fabulous "Sister Wives at the County Fair" in *Smokelong* (2018), and then I found "Let Our Bodies Be Returned to Us" on the *Wigleaf* longlist, but I know you were writing flash for years before that. Can you tell us a little about your discovery of flash? What was your first published flash story? What was the first flash you remember reading?

Thank you, Kathryn. I didn't know the term "flash fiction" when we started *100 Word Story* in 2011. I studied creative writing in college, so I probably read flash before I realized it was its own genre. But reading our very high volume of submissions to the journal intensively for years really showed me what could be done in a small space. Our first year we didn't have enough submissions, so I wrote a trio of what I called "scarytales," a hybrid of horror and fairytale, for an October issue. So, those were my first published flash pieces. After that I began writing in earnest.

You were an editor at *100 Word Story* and now edit a new(ish) hybrid journal, *Centaur*. Can you tell us something about what makes

a story speak to you? Do you know from the first line that you want to accept something, or do you sometimes need to let stories sit before you decide?

I read a submission several times or more and let it sink it. But often I can tell right away when a piece is a good match for *Centaur*. I'm not sure if I can describe it in any way but to say that it is a writer's commitment to the piece. I feel like it shows when a writer went to the bottom of the sea to create their work, and gave it their all before surfacing again with something only they could produce. It shows in not only the unique perspective, but in the layering, meticulous word choices, specific voice, and care with which a piece is polished and then shared with the journal.

Centaur **is "Home to the Hybrid." Hybridity can be so many different things; how do you see it manifesting in your own work and the pieces you publish?**

I do love hybrids that include artwork and creative formatting. As a one-woman band, I knew from the get-go that I would not be equipped to go that far in publishing hybrid work, though. And I think there are great journals already doing that. I am simply looking for pieces that may be harder to categorize, such as fiction heavy on poetry— images, metaphors, risk-taking language—or creative nonfiction that makes unexpected leaps. I like those pieces that as a reader you can't quite identify as fiction or memoir. Did that really happen to the writer? Then your answer is, Who cares? It doesn't matter!

Many of the stories in your chapbook *Let Our Bodies Be Returned to Us*, and new pieces like "The Use of Salt" (in *ette* magazine) focus on women and bodies/embodiment, on existing in a female body, all the challenges and expectations that carries, and on motherhood. Do you see this as one of your recurring themes? Are there other motifs you tend to return to?

I never set out to write about the themes you identify, but you are correct that those seem to surface a lot, especially the expectations, probably as my subconscious has grappled overall with the constant question: How can one be a good mother, writer/publisher, and breadwinner all at the same time? Lately, I am writing more creative nonfiction and a lot about the past, what I would term nostalgia. While my writing has been from a woman's perspective, the nostalgia seems to be coming to the forefront as I age and compare and contrast past with present, both my own and what I see in the world.

So many of us are trying to find the elusive work/life balance, and I know you address this in your creative nonfiction piece, "A Prayer for the Pool," in *Literary Namjooning*. How do you fit writing into your life? Do you have a dedicated writing time, or is it more a matter of seizing the opportunity when it

hits? Do you feel it's important to write every day, or are you comfortable with letting the field lie fallow sometimes?

I am an inconstant writer who deeply admires writers who set up and stick to a dedicated practice. I try not to berate myself when I take long blocks of time off, but at the same time I need to be honest with myself: The only thing stopping me from writing is me. I have written after grueling work days and when kids were running in and out of the room. The chaos and demands of life feed into writing, making it rich and authentic, and providing things to write about. I do feel that if I take off long periods, it is harder to get back into the writing zone. Lately I have a lot of energy for publishing others—which is so absorbing, creative, and satisfying in its own right—and a slower pace for my writing. That said, I've had really productive writing sessions over the past four years by occasionally taking myself away for intensive DIY solo retreats. Nowhere fancy; I go to sort of shabby one-room places with a kitchenette. I just like the uninterrupted solitude, with a pad of paper and a pen. Then I'm good to go.

Five Questions for Nadia Jacobson

WITH KATHRYN KULPA

In addition to your own writing, you are a fiction editor at Ilanot Review, a writing teacher and coach, and a founding director of WriteSpace Jerusalem, an organization for English-language writers in Jerusalem. Can you tell us a little about how the different roles influence each other? Does working with other writers help you to spot problems in your own stories, or do you need to turn off the internal editor at times so you can write freely?

As a fiction editor, I seek to showcase and amplify the reach of a story – give a story a virtual presence out in the world. It's a story to share with others. There are so many wonderful stories, so many different voices, and I want them to be heard. As a writing teacher, editor, and mentor and I help writers learn how to put their imagination on the page, shape their stories, deal with their inner critic and get out of their own way. I see all my roles as connected: helping the voices of writers get heard.

It's often much easier to spot problems in other people's work, then somewhat embarrassedly acknowledge that I do the same, here's how both of us can fix it.

I separate my editing and creating times; I even sit in different places. If I try to edit as I write, I become a perfectionist and end up writing nothing of interest.

Ilanot Review has an impressive four flash pieces in the current _Best Microfiction_. How did you come to discover flash fiction? Do you remember the first flash story you read, and when you started writing flash? I know you also write long-form fiction, but does flash have a special place in your heart?

I'm thrilled that so many of our flash pieces have been selected for the current issue of _Best Microfiction_. It's a testament to the talent of those who share their work with us. I'm very grateful that these stories will be read by an even wider audience.

Many years ago, I was introduced to the world of flash fiction by Tania Hershman, a fellow Brit and a wonderful writer — we were in a writing group together. Encapsulating a world with an emotional punch folded in very few words thrilled me, especially since I tended to write short, intense pieces and had been concerned about how to make my stories longer and to focus on one story rather than generating tiny story after tiny story (yes, I have ADHD). I was hooked.

I find flash fiction sizzles whereas a novel is a

slow burn. Both satisfying in different ways. I'm currently working on two novels that sprang from a 100-word flash. I'm experimenting with incorporating flash sections, especially for moments of intensity within my novels. I'm more apt to experiment with flash, which I find very exciting. Once I finish these novels, I'll probably go back to writing more flash.

When you read work for *Ilanot Review*, is there something that tells you right away that this is a story you're going to publish, or do some stories sneak up on you more slowly? Is there something that makes a story stand out for you, whether voice or style or subject?

Sometimes I get a little tingle or a jolt for an absolute 'yes'. Voice, style or subject matter all play a part, though voice and some form of emotional punch are paramount to me. Other times, a story that was a 'maybe' gives me a niggling feeling that draws me back to read it again, that I missed something on the first read or it's a story that takes longer to sink in.

I read first for sheer pleasure. As an editor in a journal, I have come to realise how subjective the reading of a story is. When I've had a bad night's sleep or I'm in an overly critical mood, I won't read submissions as it colours my voting.

In an interview with *The Times of Israel*, you said "A mother tongue shapes your thoughts and culture." It's fascinating to think about

how language itself shapes our thoughts. How has your experience as an immigrant affected your writing? As an editor at an international journal, do you see commonalities in the works of authors writing in English, even though they may come from different cultures?

There are certain common assumptions within language and the structure of language. Turns of phrase, idioms, for instance that only make sense within a specific cultural context. I remember my Dutch teacher in secondary school would say things like "see how the rainworm jumps" or "make love not coffee". Living here cross-language dynamics are at play; words in English, Hebrew, and Arabic pepper everyone's speech and can come out in my writing. My husband is French and speaks to the kids in his mother tongue, so I will sometimes slip into French to express that *mot juste*. As an international journal, which publishes translations as well as work originally written in English, we embrace a huge variety of cultures and storytelling forms that maintain their rich specificity.

Can you tell us about how you work writing into your daily life, along with the responsibilities of editing and teaching and managing a writing center? Do you have a dedicated writing time, or is it more a matter of seizing the opportunity when it hits? Is there a project you're working on now that you're excited about?

I'm always writing and observing. I constantly jot down characters, images, and situations in a notebook and take photos and record memos on my phone. During the workshops I lead, when everyone is working on a prompt, I write, too. To pull fragments together into fully-fledged stories and play with them, takes time. I used to create and edit stories from 10pm until 2am when my imagination crackles with energy. As you can imagine, it played havoc with family life. Instead, I try to organize my year so that I have breathing space to write, edit, create and improve my craft. I run my intensive workshops only twice a year, in May and October, for instance, and I vary the prose editing I do (fiction and non-fiction) so don't take on more than I can handle. I will also sign up for a workshop or use a journal's deadline to channel me into a burst of frenetic energy to get that story/get that chapter done. Recently, I've been dedicating a day a week to focus on my novels as my characters are fearful I'll never finish their stories! Life doesn't always work out as planned (I have kids and elderly parents to take care of), but I try my best to protect my creative time.

Best Microfiction thanks the journals where these pieces appeared in 2024.

ALL MATERIAL USED BY PERMISSION.

"I Have Lied to You" by Pamela Painter from *10 by 10*.

"Umami" by Shlagha Borah from *ANMLY*.

"Open the Door" by Mary Grimm from *Apple Valley Review*.

"Lookback Window" by Patricia Engel from *Aster(ix)*.

"Somewhere, Deep inside her Lacrimals, Something is Blocking Cora's Tears." by Hayli May Cox from *Bending Genres*.

"Plotting" by Grant Faulkner from *Boudin*.

"A Memory of Dreams, A Dream of Memories" by David Henson from *Bright Flash Literary Review*.

"Mushrooms" by Kathryn Kulpa, "The girl goes" by Cathy Ulrich, and "Manual for an American Novice in a Small Indian Town" by Tara Isabel Zambrano from *Centaur*.

"Settle" by Kathryn Kulpa from *Dirtbag*.

"Afterlife for Rent" by Kati Bumbera and "The Meaning of Words Unknown to Doug" by Karen Walker from *Does It Have Pockets*.

"Shape-shifting for beginners" by Angelita Lapuz Bradney and "River" by Claudia Monpere from *Emerge Literary Journal*.

"Spent" by Ingrid Jendrzejewski from *Every Day Fiction*.

"It Was a Year" by Kelli Short Borges from *Fictive Dream*.

"Stuck" by Karen Crawford from *Flash Boulevard*.

"Bug Facts" by Timothy Boudreau from *FlashFlood*.

"Breaking Bread" by Kim Chinquee and "Outside" by Nina Schuyler from *Ghost Parachute*.

"The Day I Went Missing" by Jessica Klimesh and "Woolworth" by Didi Wood from *Gooseberry Pie*.

"Two Girls" by Skyler Melnick from *HAD*.

"Our First Night Together" by Chelsea Stickle and "Fish Soup" by Jenny Wong from *Identity Theory*.

"Of Ducks" by Richard Leise and "Baby on the Verge" by Jenny M. Liu from *jmww*.

"Separation" by Frankie McMillan from *Landfall 248*.

"The Princess of Tides" by Amy Barnes and "Moonlit Fields" by Andrew Bertaina from *Literary Namjooning*.

"Three Hearts to Love Myself" by Elena Zhang from *Lost Balloon*.

"Without You" by Kathleen McGookey from *MacQueen's Quinterly*.

"Vandals" by Suzanne Hicks, "How to Become an Auctioneer" by Matt Leibel, and "Invisible Roads" by Janaya Young from *matchbook*.

"Mars" by Richard Holinger from *Midway Journal*.

"When She Falls" by Marie-Louise McGuinness and "The Wives" by Dawn Miller from *Milk Candy Review*.

"The Poet at Twilight" by Joshua McKinney from *MoonPark Review*.

"Motel Radio" by Lindsay Hill from *New England Review*.

"Rosetta Post-Its" by Guy Biederman and "Pet Shop Boys" by Tim Craig from *New Flash Fiction Review*.

"Valuables" by Lynn Mundell from *New World Writing Quarterly*.

"Appetites" by Emma Goldman-Sherman from *NUNUM*.

"Anya Underground" by Ryan Griffith from *Peatsmoke Journal*.

"Sea Watchers" by Sarah Freligh and "C D E F G A" by J.W. McCollum from *Pithead Chapel*.

"I Ask My Doctor Not to Pray for Me" by Nin Andrews from *Plume Poetry*.

"Self-Portrait in the Time of Disaster" by Federico Escobar from *Sad Girl Diaries*.

"Clara Schumann Washing Dishes" by Laton Carter from *Salamander*.

"Where Is Home?" by Christine H. Chen, "Mother Teaches Us to Play Tennis at Brookside Park" by Mary Grimm, "Luda, The Girl Who Was My Best Friend" by Stella Fridman Hayes, and "Forest Nuns in the Wild" by Robert Scotellaro from *South Florida Poetry Journal*.

"Forecast" by Vanessa Hua from *Split Lip Magazine*.

"Empty Nest" by Katie Humphries from *Tahoma Literary Review*.

"Laugh Track" by Will Musgrove from *The Cincinnati Review*.

"What I Can't See" by Melanie Maggard from *The Citron Review*.

"Questions The Caseworker Should Have Asked After My Ex Accused Me of Neglect" by Barbara Diggs and "Holothurian" by Addison Zeller from *The Disappointed Housewife*.

"The Incident" by Cheryl Snell from *The Ekphrastic Review*.

"Newlyweds" by Jonathan Johnson from *The Glacier*.

"Crossing Margo's Larder Off Your Bucket List" by Mikki Aronoff, "The Devil You Don't Know" by Melissa Llanes Brownlee, "Mary" by Christine H. Chen, and "You're Safe" by Avital Gad-Cykman from *The Ilanot Review*.

112 Harvard Ave #65
Claremont, CA 91711 USA

pelekinesis@gmail.com
www.pelekinesis.com

Pelekinesis titles are available through Ingram,
Gardners, directly from the publisher's website,
and at your favorite local bookstore.